PUTTING DOWN ROOTS

IN

KINSEY FALLS

GAYLE LEESON

Putting Down Roots in Kinsey Falls by Gayle Leeson
ISBN: 978-0-9967647-3-5

Chapter One

❀

"**T**HAT ONE RIGHT THERE is up to something." Greta placed a hand on her best friend Millie's arm to halt their approach to Nothin' But Knit, the knitting shop owned by Millie's granddaughter Jade and Jade's friend Terri.

"Who is?" Millie asked.

Greta nodded at the young woman currently buying red and pink variegated yarn from

Jade. The young woman who was "up to something" was standing at the counter with her back to Greta and Millie.

Millie clucked her tongue. "Ever since you started reading those cozy mysteries, you've thought *everyone* was up to something."

"Well, *she* really is. She might look all sweet and charming with that long blonde hair and that girl-next-door smile, but she doesn't have me fooled." Greta nodded. "She's hiding something. I'm sure of it."

"What makes you so certain?" Millie asked.

"I went into the business center the other day, and she immediately opened a new tab on the computer she was working at. She was looking at something, and she didn't want me to know what it was."

"Maybe—and this is a long shot—it wasn't any of your business."

"It was *too* my business! What if she's a spy or a terrorist! You just never know these days." Greta shook her head. "But whatever it is, rest assured that Greta Parker is on the case, and I will not rest until I find out what that girl is hiding."

Millie was right—the cozy mysteries Greta had been reading lately had opened up a whole new world for her. Oh, she still enjoyed her romance books, too, where the heroine's biggest worry came in the form of some hotsy-totsy rival for the hero's affections or some careless miscommunication. But these mystery books were exciting...and they'd taught Greta that she should never take anything at face value. Like Ms. Joanne Faraday...recently employed at the Kinsey Falls Living and Retail Community Center pharmacy and hiding stuff on her computer from casual passersby. Exactly *what* was the newcomer hiding? Because she *was* hiding something—Greta was sure of it—and she had every intention of sleuthing it out.

* * *

Joanne Faraday stood at the counter at Nothin' But Knit, waiting for the yarn winder to finish spinning the skein of yarn she'd purchased into a ball. She watched Jade's face as the young red-haired woman frowned slightly at something beyond Joanne's right shoulder.

"She's behind me, isn't she?" Joanne asked.

"Who?" Jade asked, directing her gaze back at Joanne.

"The crazy woman with the plum-colored hair who's been stalking me for the past two days."

Jade smiled. "That's Greta, and she's heading this way with my grandmother, Millie. Greta can be a little eccentric, but I think you'll like her when you get to know her."

Joanne wasn't so sure. The woman had sneaked up on her in the business center the day before yesterday and had nearly given Joanne a heart attack. Nosy old ladies in soft-soled shoes should be declared a menace to society.

The plum-haired woman and her sophisticated-looking, silver-haired friend entered the shop.

"Hi," Jade said, brightly. "I'd like you guys to meet Joanne Faraday. Joanne, this is my grandmother, Millie, and her friend Greta."

"Nice to meet you." Joanne could certainly see the resemblance between Jade and Millie. The two shared the same beautiful bone structure and striking green eyes. Joanne felt a pang. She'd been adopted as a baby and had no idea who she might look like.

"What brings you guys to the shop?" Jade asked.

"Greta was heading this way, and I thought I'd join her and ask if you and Caleb would like to join me for dinner and a movie tonight—my treat."

"I'd planned to go with Millie, but something came up." Greta ventured a glance toward Terri, who was restocking the yarn bins. Terri was bound to have heard Greta, but she kept poking yarn into the cubbies as if she hadn't.

"That sounds great, Grandma," Jade said. "I'll check with Caleb to make sure that works for him." Jade turned to Joanne. "It's actually because of Grandma that my boyfriend and I met." She laughed. "Sometimes, I think he likes her as much as he does me."

"Pish tosh," Millie said.

"That's tellin' 'em," Greta said.

Nothin' But Knit was a charming shop. The right part of the store was for the merchandise: yarn, knitting needles, crochet hooks, yarn needles, stitch markers, pattern books, and looms. Near the window, there was a navy padded bench. There was a knitting room to the left with a large, round white table. The chairs nestled around the table had purple-and pink-paisley cushions. It was a cozy, friendly room in which to work.

Joanne's yarn finished winding, and Jade took the ball off the spool. She handed the yarn to Joanne, who thanked her, and said, "Back to the knitting room."

"I have a lightweight shawl I'd like to work on," Greta says.

"I can get that for you." Terri followed Greta into the knitting room, where there were sixteen cabinets. Most of the cabinets were labeled with the names of regular customers who liked to keep projects in the cabinets when they weren't working on them. For residents of the Kinsey Falls Living and Retail Community Center, it helped keep their micro-apartments from getting cluttered with works in progress.

"I believe I'll sit here beside you," Greta announced, putting her knitting on the table next to Joanne.

There was no one else seated at the table, so Greta could have sat in any of the seven other empty chairs, but why would Joanne have expected Greta to sit anywhere expect right beside her?

* * *

Before getting down to some serious sleuthing, Greta went over to the cabinet to talk with Terri. She'd been dating Terri's uncle, Steve, and Terri wasn't too happy about it. Greta didn't know why. Maybe it was because Terri was afraid that a free spirit like Greta would break Steve's reserved heart. But Greta had no intention of hurting Steve. They made compromises. Tonight, they were doing something he wanted to do, and tomorrow night, Steve would take her dancing.

"Steve is taking me to something called a Ted talk tonight," Greta told Terri.

"That's nice."

Greta was eager to let Terri know how much she was working to make Steve happy. "I don't know who this Ted is or what he'll be talking about, but Steve seems to think we'll enjoy it."

Terri just shook her head before leaving the knitting room.

"Thanks," Greta called.

"You're welcome."

Greta sat down beside Joanne and sighed. "I'm dating Terri's uncle, and Terri's mad at me over it. We used to get along really well—I introduced Terri to some of my YP friends—you know, the young professionals who live upstairs?"

"I am one of the YPs," Joanne said. "I live upstairs, and I work at the pharmacy."

The Community Center provided micro-apartments to both seniors—dubbed golden oldies—and young professionals in the upper level of a renovated shopping mall. The bottom level was retail space. Residents had virtually everything they needed in one central location. There were even vegetable gardens—one for the seniors, and one for the YPs—on either side of the building.

"Have you been dating Terri's uncle long?" Joanne asked.

"We started seeing each other after the Community Center's grand opening celebration about a month and a half ago. Until then, Terri liked me. Now…" Greta shrugged.

"For the record, a TED Talk is a forum where different people speak. The *T* stands for *Technology*, the *E* is for *Entertainment*, and the *D* is for *Design*. You can look up TED Talks online, if you'd like to familiarize yourself with them before your date."

"So, Ted isn't a person?"

Joanne shook her head.

Greta sighed. "That's why Terri doesn't want me to date Steve. She thinks I'm not sophisticated enough." She was letting the conversation be all about her when it needed to be about Joanne. She decided to steer the conversation back in the right direction. "Thanks for telling me. You said you work at the pharmacy?"

"Yep. I'm a pharmacy tech."

"Do you like that work?"

"I do." Joanne seemed determined to concentrate on her knitting.

Greta could happily knit and interrogate her suspect at the same time. "What made you decide to live here?"

Joanne shrugged. "There was an apartment available, and it was convenient."

"No, I mean here in Kinsey Falls. Are you from here?"

"No. But I came for a visit, and Kinsey Falls struck me as a nice place to put down roots."

"You know, I couldn't help but notice that when Jade and Millie were talking, you got a funny look on your face. It made me think maybe you and your grandmother don't get along so well."

"I...um...I've never had a grandmother," Joanne said, eyes still on her knitting. "My parents were older when they adopted me. They'd put their careers ahead of starting a family until it was too late for them to have children of their own. And their parents were dead by the time I came along."

"I'm sorry. Are your parents still living?"

"My father is...but his dementia has progressed to the stage where he doesn't know me anymore."

Greta was on the verge of hugging the young woman—suspect or not—when Joanne flung her knitting onto the table in disgust.

"I'll never get the hang of this," she said.

"Let me see." Greta picked up the knitting and examined it. "Oh, this is all right. You just twisted a stitch. We can go back and fix it." She unraveled the row until she was past the twisted stitch. Then she deftly got Joanne back to the place where she was when she'd noticed the mistake. "Just check your knitting every row or two to make sure the stitches are falling correctly. That way you can catch any mishaps before they get out of hand."

"Thanks, Ms. Parker."

"It's Greta...and you're welcome."

* * *

Greta was out of breath when she arrived for the book club meeting at the Violet Room. Each of the Community Center's common rooms were named for a flower. The Violet Room was the smallest, and it was tastefully decorated in shades of purple, mauve, and white. The other meeting rooms were the Sunflower, Rose, and Gladiolus.

"I'm sorry I'm late." Greta looked around the room and confirmed that she was, as she'd thought, the last to arrive. Gilda and her jug—a small brown, bug-eyed dog that was a cross between a pug and a Jack Russell terrier—named Moonshine sat on the white wicker chair to the right of the fireplace. Mabel sat on the rocker to the other side of the hearth, and Judy, Opal, and Sue sat on the long sofa.

They all murmured greetings, and even Moonshine let out a happy yip.

Greta sat on the ottoman across from the sofa and somewhat between Gilda and Mabel. As she dropped her tote onto the floor beside her, she said, "As good as *The Murder of Roger Ackroyd* is, I've got a real-life mystery that needs to be solved."

Gilda readjusted Moonshine on her lap and leaned forward. "What kind of mystery?"

"There's a new girl who showed up in Kinsey Falls just out of the blue. She was in the business center the other day, and when I walked past, she opened a new tab so I couldn't see what she was doing." Greta looked around to see everybody's reaction.

Mabel looked confused. Sue appeared to be irritated. And Opal, Gilda, and Judy were thoughtful. Moonshine didn't give two hoots unless there was a treat in it for him. There wasn't. At least, not unless he could find out what Joanne was doing.

"So what?" Sue asked. "She probably figured that whatever she was doing was none of your business."

Knowing how envious Sue was of Millie, and that her envy usually manifested in not liking anything about Millie, Greta said, "That's exactly what Millie said."

Sue's eyes widened, and she drew in a breath. "On the other hand, if this girl was acting *sneaky*, then it could be all of our business."

"What do you mean, Sue?" Judy crossed her thick ankles. "You don't think this girl aims to blow up the building, do you?"

"Well, of course, I'm not saying that at all." Sue flattened her lips and glared at Judy momentarily before adding, "But I'm not *not* saying that either."

"I believe what Sue is saying is that we—as a group of amateur sleuths—should find out what this young woman is doing here in Kinsey Falls," Greta said.

"Right." Sue gave an emphatic nod.

"I'm no amateur sleuth," Judy said. "I get all the excitement I can handle when my grandchildren visit."

Opal scoffed. "My daughter thinks I get my grandchildren *too* excited. I say we all need some adventure in our lives."

"Your daughter just doesn't want her children riding with you on that screaming metal death trap," Sue said.

"Pinky is a motorcycle, and I drive her responsibly."

Pinky was, in fact, a motorcycle with a sidecar, and Greta wouldn't have sworn that Opal was always the most responsible driver. But the Silver Sleuths only had the room for an hour, and she didn't want Sue and Opal to spend it bickering. "Let's not forget about our mystery."

"Right," Mabel piped up. "We're here to discuss the murder of Dan Aykroyd."

"Not Dan Aykroyd, Mabel," Judy said. "Roger Ackroyd."

"I don't know him." Mabel wrinkled her forehead. "Was he on *Saturday Night Live* too?" She looked so earnest that not even Sue had the heart to correct her.

"Mabel's right." Gilda smoothed Moonshine's ears. "We should go ahead and talk about Ms. Christie's book...and then whoever wants to can meet later to discuss the other mystery."

Chapter Two

❀

AFTER GRETA HAD LEFT the business center, Joanne had searched for people who might've been in her mother's graduating high school class. She'd found a group on social media and sent private messages to a few of the members. It wasn't much, but it was something. She'd wished she had someone in whom she could confide. More than anyone, she wanted to tell her dad. She missed him terribly. No, he wasn't actually gone yet, and Joanne visited him every chance she got...but he wasn't the man she'd grown up with.

She wandered over to the café and ordered a burger, fries, and a milkshake. When she received her food, she took her tray over to a table by the window.

A pretty brunette walked past and did a double-take at Joanne's food choices. Joanne cringed slightly, but she owed no one an explanation about what she was eating or why.

The brunette sat down across from Joanne. "Hi. I'm Kelsey. Are you all right?"

"I'm fine. Why?"

"In my experience, that's a breakup meal," she said, nodding toward the plate. "Did you get dumped?"

"No. You're observant, though. I'll give you that."

"Wanna talk about it?"

Rather than telling this stranger everything that was happening in her life, Joanne simply told Kelsey about her dad's condition.

"Oh, wow. That's so sad. I'm sorry." Kelsey covered one of Joanne's hands with her own.

A handsome guy came into the café, walked over to their table, and tugged a strand of Kelsey's hair. "Hey, KK."

"Hi, Andrew." Kelsey slid over, so Andrew could sit beside her in the booth. "Andrew, this is…"

"Joanne." She smiled and shook his hand. "Kelsey and I just met."

"Right," Kelsey said, "and she needs some cheering up."

"Cool. What do you want to do?" Andrew included both of them in his question.

"Oh, no," Joanne said. "I wouldn't dream of intruding on your date."

The couple laughed.

"As if," Andrew said. "I'm way out of her league."

"Ha! I'm out of your league!" Kelsey playfully punched Andrew's shoulder. "This jerk is my brother."

"Mom makes me come over here and check on little KK every few days," he said.

"Where do you live?" Joanne asked him.

"Oh, I live across town. Mom and Dad, on the other hand, moved to Florida when Dad retired." He looked toward the counter. "I'm going to grab some food. What do you want?"

Kelsey asked for a chef's salad.

"Suit yourself," Andrew said. "I'm having what Joanne's having."

"You're lucky to have such a caring family," Joanne told Kelsey, while sneaking a peek at Andrew's broad back as he stood at the counter.

"He is a looker, huh?" Kelsey shook her head. "As much as I hate to admit it. And, in case you're wondering—which I believe you are—he is single. But, I warn you, he refuses to get serious about anyone until he's established himself as a corporate attorney, so...you know...tread carefully."

"I'm not looking for romance," Joanne said, thinking her heart probably couldn't take any more abuse right now anyway.

But as she watched Andrew standing in line, he caught her eye and winked at her. Joanne smiled and blushed.

"I can see that," Kelsey said.

"Well, I might not be looking for happily-ever-after...but I wouldn't mind dating a prince." She groaned as Greta and two other golden oldies walked into the café.

In a move that could only have been more inconspicuous if Greta had pointed and yelled, "There's Joanne Faraday," Greta widened her eyes and jerked her head toward Joanne's table while seemingly trying to point that way with her eyebrows. Yep. Subtlety, thy name is Greta.

Kelsey leaned across the table. "What is it?" Then her gaze traveled to the newcomers. "Hey, Greta! Come meet Joanne!"

Greta traipsed on over with her friends in tow. "Hello again, Joanne."

"Hello."

"I'd like you to meet my friends Opal and Sue." Greta made introductions all around.

"It's nice to meet you both," Kelsey said. "I'd love to have you check out one of my yoga classes to see if it appeals to you. First one's on the house." She turned back to Joanne. "That goes for you, too, of course." She swung her head around to take a closer look at Opal. "Hey! Aren't you the woman who drives that cool pink motorcycle with the sidecar?"

"That's me." Opal beamed. "Anytime you want to go for a spin, give me a holler. I love to ride."

"We should get our coffees and go on out to be with Gilda before she gives up on us," Sue said.

"Why didn't she come in?" Kelsey asked.

"She can't bring Moonshine into the café." Sue acted as if that declaration should be obvious.

"And Gilda doesn't go anywhere without her Moonshine," Opal added.

"Moonshine is Gilda's jug." Greta seemed to believe that her statement should clear everything up, but one look at Kelsey showed Joanne that the other girl still felt just as bewildered as she.

Joanne gave the women an exaggerated blink. "If your friend won't go anywhere without her jug of moonshine, don't you think she might have a problem?"

"Not *of* moonshine," Greta said, with a smile. "The jug *is* Moonshine. He's her dog."

"She thinks her jug is a dog," Joanne said.

Greta spread her hands. "Moonshine is a Jack Russell and pug mix. Therefore, he's a jug. A little brown jug to be exact."

She and her friends dissolved into a fit of laughter at this.

"See?" Opal nodded toward the hallway in front of the café where Gilda stood waiting with her arms full of Moonshine.

When she saw them all looking in their direction, Gilda lifted Moonshine's little paw and waved. Moonshine licked Gilda's nose.

"Unbelievable," Joanne said.

"Aw, he didn't do that on his own," Sue said, misconstruing what Joanne found unbelievable. "It was Gilda making him wave."

"Sue's right about us needing to get our coffee and hit the bricks, though," Greta said. "Moonshine isn't that heavy, but he can start to take a toll on you after a few minutes."

The women said goodbye and went to get their coffee. It wasn't until after they'd walked away that Joanne spoke again.

"They're...I mean, they seem...kinda crazy."

Kelsey laughed. "I know! Aren't they the best? I hope I'm eccentric like that when I get old. Don't you?"

Joanne shrugged. "They're really...out there."

"I know, but trust me, you'll love them—or Greta, at least—once you get to get to know them."

It was the second time today that Joanne had heard a similar sentiment, but she still wasn't buying it.

Andrew returned to the table with his and Kelsey's food. "What did I miss?"

* * *

Greta handed Gilda a decaf cappuccino. Gilda managed to hold Moonshine's face far enough away to get a sip.

"Hand him here," Opal said.

Gilda gladly handed the dog over, and Opal tucked him under her arm.

"What now?" Sue asked.

"Let's sit on these benches near the café. That way we can see what's going on." Greta sat where she could keep an eye on Joanne. "I'm glad Joanne has met Kelsey. That young lady finds out everything she can about everybody. She's a good one to have on our side."

"Can we be sure she's on our side?" Gilda took Moonshine's leash out of her tote and hooked it to his collar.

"Positive," Greta said.

Opal sat Moonshine on the floor, and he went from person to person to get his head patted.

"Now that we know who we're investigating," Opal said, "what's next?"

"I'm simply going to try to keep my eyes on her until I find out what she's up to." Greta sighed. "She seems like a sweet person...but, you know, Ann Rule thought Ted Bundy was a sweet person."

"Hey, there Moonshine!"

The four women turned to see Justin approaching with two bags of groceries.

"He's so handsome," Sue said.

"And smart," Gilda added. "I'd love to introduce him to my granddaughter."

He stopped, transferred both bags to one hand, and gave Moonshine a scratch on the head. Then his smile encompassed the group. "Hi, ladies. Have you had a good day?"

"We have, darlin'," Greta said. "Have you?"

"Yes, ma'am. And seeing you makes it even better." He lifted the bags a bit higher. "I'm ready to try those crepes again. I have everything I need."

"Okay. See you tomorrow morning then."

* * *

As they ate, Joanne learned that Kelsey was a dance and yoga instructor and that she owned the gym there at the Kinsey Falls Living and Retail Community Center.

"Did you see the dance Kelsey and her troupe did with that cool older woman at the grand opening celebration?" Andrew asked.

Joanne hadn't seen it. She'd been playing bingo and had won a gift basket from Nothin' But Knit, but she wasn't about to admit that to Andrew and Kelsey. They probably thought bingo was lame. "I completely missed the dance competition."

"Well, there was a lot going on that day," Kelsey said. "But anyway, the cool older woman Andrew is talking about is Greta Parker." She looked at Andrew. "She was in here just a few minutes ago. Didn't you see her?"

"No, I'm sorry to say, I didn't."

"Greta is teaching me how to cook, and she's also promised to help me learn to knit." Kelsey laughed. "Greta calls knitting *productive fidgeting.*"

Joanne joined in her new friend's laughter. "Productive fidgeting. I like that."

Andrew took a swig of his milkshake. "KK is on a big self-improvement kick to impress this guy named Justin. He—"

Kelsey bumped him with her shoulder. "Andrew, I am not. Any opportunity to improve oneself is never wasted…whether it impresses anyone else or not."

"Um…Kelsey, you're beautiful, you own your own business, you teach yoga and dance—I think you're pretty impressive already," Joanne said.

"I knew the instant I saw you sitting here that you and I were going to be great friends," Kelsey said with a grin.

"What do you do, Joanne?" Andrew asked.

"I'm a pharmacy technician here at the Community Center. What about you?"

"I'm a corporate lawyer. I spend my days drafting or reviewing boring contracts."

Kelsey scoffed at her brother. "You love every minute of it."

"I do enjoy it." He leaned back in the booth and pushed his plate away. "Who's up for a round of mini-golf?"

As Joanne, Kelsey, and Andrew were leaving the café, Kelsey gasped as she spotted a sandy-haired man carrying two reusable shopping bags approaching the stairs.

"Justin!" Kelsey called.

The young man stopped, smiled at Kelsey, and the two began walking toward each other. Joanne and Andrew followed Kelsey.

"We're on our way to play mini-golf," Kelsey said. "Wanna make it a foursome?"

"Yeah, sure." Justin nodded to Andrew. "Hey, man, how've you been?"

"Good. Keeping busy. You?"

"Same."

"Justin, this is Joanne Faraday," Kelsey said. "Joanne, this is Justin Holmes."

"Nice to meet you." He turned back to Kelsey. "Let me run

upstairs and put away my groceries, and I'll be right back."

"I'll help you." Kelsey lifted and dropped one toned shoulder. "It'll be quicker."

Kelsey and Justin hurried up the stairs, and Andrew turned to Joanne. "What do you say? You wanna ditch 'em?"

"No!" She laughed. "You wouldn't really do that, would you?"

"No. Besides, there's only one mini-golf course around here. KK would know exactly where to find us." He sighed and shook his head.

"What is it?"

"She's crazy about that guy, but he's never even taken her out on a date," Andrew said. "He says it's because he doesn't want a serious relationship until he's become successful in business."

Joanne thought that excuse sounded much like the one Kelsey said Andrew used to avoid getting tied down.

* * *

When Kelsey had approached Justin, the Silver Sleuths had wandered several feet away. But Gilda had turned up her hearing aids.

"They're going to play mini-golf," she reported.

Opal interlaced her fingers and stretched out her arms. "Who's up for eighteen holes?"

"Eighteen?" Gilda frowned. "I don't know that Moonshine and I can go that many rounds, but I can at least play nine, and then we can sit on a bench near our suspect and eavesdrop."

"I'm out," Greta said. "I have a date with Steve tonight."

The other three looked at Sue. It took a few seconds, but she finally caved.

"Fine, I'll go. But I don't want to stay out too long in the night air. If I do, my hair will be flatter than a flitter for church tomorrow."

* * *

Joanne, Kelsey, Andrew, and Justin were choosing their putters when a motorcycle roared into the parking lot. Joanne glanced over her shoulder. When she saw that the motorcycle was pink and that an older woman with cottony white hair peeking from beneath her helmet was sitting astride the machine, she turned completely to fully take it in. Joanne wasn't alone in her gawking, as everyone in the vicinity had paused to take a gander.

As if a mature woman on a pink motorcycle wasn't spectacle enough, there in the matching side car was a diminutive woman wearing a large sparkly silver helmet and holding a dog who wore goggles and the tiniest black helmet Joanne had ever seen. The women removed their helmets—and the dainty one removed the dog's.

Joanne turned to Kelsey. "Do Opal and Greta enjoy mini-golf?"

"Apparently...although that's not Greta. That's Gilda. Greta had a date with Steve tonight."

"Right," Joanne said. "The TED Talks."

"Oh, there's the other one. Sue was her name." Kelsey smiled and waved at the women.

Joanne watched as Sue emerged from a luxury SUV. "What are the odds?"

"I know! Isn't it fantastic?" Kelsey called to the women, "Come join us!"

"We don't want to horn in," Sue said, closing the gap between them.

"We're just now starting, and the more the merrier. Right, guys?"

Justin and Andrew seemed fine with the additional players, so Joanne merely smiled and nodded.

When Opal, Gilda, and the dog had joined them, Justin clucked the dog under the chin.

"Hello, Moonshine."

The dog wagged its tail so hard, Gilda could barely hold him. Opal had to get its leash out of Gilda's tote, so they could hook him to it and let him down. As soon as he was free, he danced around Justin's feet.

Kelsey and Justin seemed to know—and like—many of the

golden oldies...Justin even more so than Kelsey. Joanne wondered if it was because maybe Justin's business—whatever it was; she didn't think she'd heard anyone say—was geared toward older clients. Or maybe he was simply outgoing. At face value, Kelsey certainly was friendly. She'd made it her mission that evening to keep Joanne from wallowing in self-pity. But why?

It was hard for Joanne to accept kindness without questioning it. It had been her unfortunate experience that, except for her parents, most people were nice to you because they wanted something.

* * *

Greta wore a simple emerald-green knee-length sheath, nude kitten-heel pumps, a long silver pendant, and matching earrings. Thank goodness, her best friend lived just next door. Leaving her front door unlocked, she hurried over and knocked on Millie's door.

"Millie, it's me. I need you to zip my dress."

Millie opened the door. "Turn around."

Greta did as instructed, and Millie zipped her up.

"Gorgeous! That man won't know what hit him."

"I hope so," Greta said.

"You don't sound so sure of yourself. What's wrong?"

"Has Jade said anything to you about how Terri feels about my dating Steve?"

"No," Millie said, "Jade hasn't mentioned it."

Greta squinted at her. "Is that true, or are you just trying to spare my feelings?"

"It's true. Why?"

"Things have changed between Terri and me since I started dating her uncle. I felt we were getting to be good friends until here lately." Greta shrugged. "Now, she shuts me down every time I try to talk with her. And the only thing that's changed is that I'm dating Steve."

"Well, why don't you and Steve arrange a double date with Terri and Mitch Reedy?"

Mitch was a field reporter for a local television station. Terri and Mitch had been out on occasion since the Kinsey Falls Living and Retail Community Center's grand opening celebration. Mitch had covered the event for the news.

"A double date would give Terri the opportunity to see how good for each other you and Steve are," Millie continued.

"That's not a bad idea. I'll run it by Steve this evening." She gave Millie a quick hug. "Thanks for everything. I'll see you later."

Less than five minutes after Greta got back to her apartment, Steve arrived. He wore khakis, a light-blue button-down shirt open at the throat, and a navy sport coat. His thick hair was more salt than pepper, he had blue eyes that often held a mischievous glint, and he had an athletic build.

Steve kissed her, drew her in for a long hug, and then kissed her again. "You look incredible."

"Thanks. You look awfully good yourself."

Greta's husband Ray had been tall and skinny. She'd loved Ray very much, but she'd never felt as safe and sheltered in his arms as she did in Steve's.

He checked his watch. "We'd better get going."

"Yes. I don't want to miss any of the speakers on technology, education, and design." She glanced at him sideways to see if he was impressed that she knew exactly what they were going to hear, but if he was, he hid it well.

On the drive to the library, Greta was uncharacteristically quiet. Her mind was on several things: Joanne Faraday, how the Silver Sleuths were doing—good, she hoped, but not *too* good without her—and Terri.

"What's the matter?" Steve asked.

Greta chose the topic that was pertinent to him. "I'm thinking about Terri. I don't believe she likes that we're dating."

"I don't remember asking her permission," Steve said.

"I know, but you're her favorite uncle. And she and I were just getting friendly."

"Do you want me to talk with her?"

"No...that wouldn't help. She'd only resent me for causing trouble between you."

She told him about Millie's double-date idea. "What do you think?"

Steve instructed the car to call Terri.

"What? No! Wait...what are you doing?"

He ignored the woman panicking beside him as Terri answered the call. "Hey, munchkin, are you free for dinner tomorrow?"

"Yes."

"Good. You and Mitch meet Greta and me at Sherman's Steakhouse at five o'clock."

"Um...Mitch might have to work, Uncle Steve."

"Well, either way, we'll look forward to seeing you. Let me know if you need a ride. Love you!" He ended the call and winked at Greta.

Chapter Three

❀

JOANNE YAWNED AND STRETCHED, then smiled as she remembered last night. Gorgeous Andrew…what a wonderful man. He'd been funny, charming, smart, sexy…what more could a woman want?

She turned and gazed at his face—eyelashes long enough to inspire any woman's envy, full lips that were slightly parted in his sleep. She leaned over and pressed a kiss into his bare shoulder. He stirred, snaked an arm around her and said, "You can do better than that."

The alarm went off, and Joanne bolted upright. She instinctively looked at the other side of her bed—barely disturbed—to make sure she'd been dreaming. She buried her face in her hands, certain that if she could see herself, she'd be blushing.

She and Andrew had exchanged numbers at the end of the evening, but Joanne didn't hold out much hope that he'd call her. Even if he did, she probably shouldn't answer. Getting involved with Andrew Dennison would be one more heartbreak waiting to happen. When she'd told Kelsey she wasn't looking for happily-ever-after and wouldn't mind dating a prince, Joanne hadn't known how much she'd like her new friend's brother.

She told herself again that if Andrew called she probably shouldn't take the call...but, of course, she would.

She got out of bed and wandered into the kitchen for some breakfast. She readied the coffee pot and put two slices of bread into the toaster. As she waited for her coffee to brew and her toast to pop up, she looked around her kitchen.

It was a pretty little kitchen, all clean and white. When her mother had been alive, their kitchen had always been...not cluttered exactly...but full. Her mother had adored cookbooks and had dozens. She'd tried to grow her own herbs—it was hit and miss—on the windowsill. The countertops had been cluttered with appliances— blender, mixer, food processor, waffle iron, convection oven, slow cooker. Other than the toaster, the can opener, and the coffeemaker, Joanne's counters were bare. She hadn't brought a single one of her mother's cookbooks from home. She couldn't...not yet. She couldn't bring herself to even look at them. Even though Mom had been gone over a year, it was still too soon.

Joanne caught sight of her reflection in the door of the microwave. Though the image was distorted, she could see that her pajamas hung on her as if she were a scarecrow. She'd found grief to be an excellent diet aid, although she'd never been overweight. Maybe she could join one of Kelsey's classes and get toned...or at least reap some of the relaxing benefits of yoga.

She wondered briefly if coming to Kinsey Falls had been a mistake. So far, all she'd discovered was that her birth mother, whose name was Carla Crockett, was dead. Not that Carla would have wanted Joanne in her life had she been living. Carla's parents— Joanne's biological grandparents—had certainly wanted nothing to do with her. They'd seen her as a painful reminder of what they'd lost.

And what about those crazy old ladies? Granted, they'd sure made the mini-golf game livelier, but they'd asked Joanne a lot of questions. *What brought you to Kinsey Falls? What kind of work do you do? Do you see yourself sticking around, or are you here just for a while?* Were they that nosy with everyone, or was it just her?

* * *

Greta had just tied her Wonder Woman apron around her waist when Justin knocked on her door. "Hidey-ho, darlin'! Do you need an apron? I have a Marilyn Monroe apron you can wear, or you can wear this one, and I'll take Marilyn."

"I'm good," Justin said. "I'm not really an apron kinda guy."

"I know, but I don't want you to get your clothes messed up."

He grinned. "I'll take my chances."

"So…the crepes. Are you ready?"

Justin handed Greta the bag he'd brought into the kitchen. "I think so. I believe I got everything we'll need."

"If you didn't, I probably have it." She winked. "You didn't have to go out and buy your own ingredients, you know."

"Sure, I did. You provide the ingredients and the lessons all the time."

Greta started unpacking the bag. "Okay, good. You got flour, eggs, milk, and butter. I've got the sugar and the vanilla extract. We're good to go." She got out a mixing bowl. "Did you have a good time at mini-golf last night?"

"Yeah, it was fun." He frowned. "Wait. How'd you know I played mini-golf last night?"

Ooops. "Um…Opal."

"Oh, yeah. Kelsey hadn't met Opal, Sue, and Gilda before. She really liked them."

"What about you?" Gilda took a set of measuring cups and spoons out of the cabinet.

"Sure. They're great."

"How about Kelsey? You two seem close."

"Kelsey's a really sweet girl." He narrowed his baby blues at her. "Where are you going with this, Greta?"

"Just wondering if you and Kelsey are an item, that's all." She smiled.

"Well, we're not...not right now anyway. But that doesn't mean I'm interested in Opal." He laughed. "So, don't go trying to matchmake."

"You'd better not be. If you were interested in *any* of the golden oldies, it had better be me."

"You know it would be."

"Why *aren't* you and Kelsey an item?" Greta asked. "You seem to get along so well together."

"I don't want to get serious about anyone until I'm secure in my career. I want to have...you know...made it before I settle down."

"That's wonderful, darlin', but just don't let somebody else come along and sweep her off her feet while she's waiting for you."

"All right. Now, about those crepes..."

Greta saw that she wasn't going to get anything more out of Justin about Kelsey, so she opened the flour and changed the subject. "What did you think of that new girl—Joanne, I believe her name is?"

"She was okay." Justin tore off a piece of waxed paper to put on the table before they got started so that cleanup would be a snap. Greta had taught him well. "You know how Kelsey is—she saw Joanne sitting in the café looking all down in the dumps and made it her mission to cheer her up."

"Did it work?"

"Seemed to. I got the impression she was really into Kelsey's brother Andrew."

"Well, good. It's nice that she's making some friends. I don't think she's been in Kinsey Falls very long."

Justin measured out one and three-fourths cups of flour and sifted it into the mixing bowl. "She told Kelsey she moved here about two months ago. Her dad has dementia. That's what she was depressed about."

"That's sad."

He cracked an egg into the bowl. "Yeah. She said something about having to put him in a long-term care facility." He added two more eggs. "You said you prefer a mixer to a whisk, right?"

"For crepes, I do. We don't want there to be any lumps in our batter." She wondered if Joanne's appearance in Kinsey Falls had anything to do with her father's being put in a long-term care facility. Maybe she moved here to be closer to him… Or maybe she believes that someone or something—like a factory—caused her father's condition. If so, she could be out for revenge.

She realized Justin had said something. "What, sweetie?"

"How's this looking so far?"

"It looks wonderful. You're doing a terrific job."

"Yeah…I did last time, too, until it came time to flip them," he said.

"You'll get it this time—I'm sure of it."

* * *

Before going to work, Joanne went down to the business center and logged onto the social media site on which she'd sent messages to people who'd gone to school with her mother. Her heart raced when she saw that one of the women had responded.

Angela Wilson Hazelton had said, *Oh, my goodness! I didn't even know Carla had a daughter! She was my best friend all throughout school. I was so sorry to hear that she'd died. You say you're looking for your father. Well, she was head over heels in love with Robert Parker, so he could very well have been your dad. They were a terrific couple…they'd planned to get married.*

Joanne saw that Angela was online, so she wrote back: *What happened between them?*

Angela responded, *Robert died in a car accident. Poor Carla fell apart when it happened.*

I'm so sorry, she wrote. How different her life might've been had

Robert not died. *Do you think he was my father?*

This reply was slower in coming. *I'm not sure. Not long after Robert's death, Carla got involved with someone she worked with.*

She'd gotten involved with someone she worked with? Had it been so easy for her mother to forget the guy she supposedly loved? *Who?*

His name was Winston Wallace. He worked in a law firm there in Kinsey Falls.

Neither Joanne nor Angie responded for several minutes. Finally, Angela added: *I'm sorry. I hope you find what you're looking for.*

* * *

Greta was pleased when she hurried down the stairs to meet the Silver Sleuths in front of the pharmacy. For one thing, Justin had done well with his crepes. They were light, thin, crispy, and delicious. They'd put strawberry jam and whipped cream on them and had a wonderful breakfast.

The other reason Greta was self-satisfied was because Justin had given her a few details about Joanne. That way, even though she wasn't at mini-golf with the other Sleuths, she wasn't entirely in the dark.

Sue loved to know stuff that she didn't think anyone else knew. Then she'd either dole it out little by little or make you come right out and ask her. Well, today, when Sue started throwing out her crumbs of information, Greta would be able to come out with a cookie of her own, thanks to Justin.

Opal and Sue were sitting on a bench in front of the pharmacy.

"Where's Gilda?" Greta asked.

"She went to the pet shop to pick up a few things for Moonshine," Opal said.

Sue rolled her eyes. "She said she wanted to make it look like she was shopping by actually doing some shopping."

"That's not a bad strategy." Greta looked over her shoulder at the pharmacy. "Have you seen anybody suspicious-looking talking with Joanne?"

"No," Opal said, "but she did go to the business center before work."

"I wonder what she's doing there that she can't do on or phone or her own laptop or tablet?" Greta asked.

"Well, lots of things if she doesn't want it traced back to her." Sue gave a solemn nod.

"That's a good point," Greta said. "That's a *really* good point. What could she *not* want traced back to her?"

"How to build a bomb," Opal suggested.

"How to rob a bank," Sue said.

They looked at each other and said almost simultaneously, "How to build a bomb to blow up a bank vault!"

"That could be it." Greta leaned against a column. "Justin told me this morning that Joanne's father has been put in a dementia facility. Maybe she needs money to pay for his care."

"It's expensive, that's for sure." Opal shook her head. "My sister-in-law had to sell everything her mother had to pay the nursing home."

"Well, if the poor girl needs money, then we could have a benefit for her or something. She doesn't have to rob a bank."

Gilda and Moonshine arrived just in time to hear the end of Greta's sentence. "Who's robbing a bank? Not us, I hope."

"No, Gilda," Sue said. "It's not us."

"But we think it might be Joanne." Opal leaned forward and patted Moonshine's head. "Justin told Greta that she had to put her dad in long-term care."

"Bless her little ol' heart." Gilda looked at the floor. "I hope we don't ever have to go to one of those, don't you, Moonshine?"

The dog panted up at her, his tongue hanging sideways out of his mouth. Apparently, they had some sort of telepathic communication because Gilda said, "Of course, I'd never go anywhere without you. You're my sweet boy."

"I was saying that if we knew for certain that's what Joanne was planning, then we could talk her out of it," Greta said. "We can come up with other ways to help her out...like a bake sale."

"But how can we be sure, short of asking her?" Sue raised a fingertip to her lips but didn't actually nibble the nail. She used to be a nail-biter, and even though she'd broken the habit, she still put her fingers near her mouth when she was thinking.

"For one thing, we need to be in that business center every time we see her going in there."

Greta knew Opal was right about that, but Joanne was bound to get around them sometimes. "Let me feel her out a little bit." She nodded at her companions and strolled into the pharmacy.

* * *

Joanne pinched the bridge of her nose between her forefinger and thumb and closed her eyes. When she opened them, Greta was still coming straight at her. She tried to look busy, but unfortunately, there was no one at the pharmacy counter at that moment.

"Hidey-ho!" Greta gave her a little wave. "How are you this morning?"

"I'm fine, thanks. How are you, Greta?"

"I'm doing well. I should probably go to the bank before they close today. Are you familiar with the Kinsey Falls Bank?"

Joanne nodded. "I recently opened an account there."

"It's really nice, don't you think? Not very big, though. I doubt it takes in a lot of money." She leaned closer. "I certainly don't think it would be worth robbing. Do you?"

"Are you asking me if I think the Kinsey Falls Bank would be worth robbing?" Joanne's whisper came out as an incredulous hiss.

"Well, you know...those heist movies are popular...but I don't believe you could pay even George Clooney and Brad Pitt with the money you'd get from Kinsey Falls Bank, much less those little acrobats that get in the vault and stuff."

"Acrobats?"

"Yeah…haven't you seen the movie?"

"Apparently, I haven't. But Ms. Par—" *Parker.* "Ms. Parker…Greta Parker."

Greta frowned. "What is it? You can tell me. Maybe I can help."

"I…I can't go into it right now, but can we talk later? About one, maybe? That's when I take my lunch break."

"Sure, darlin'. Would you like to come up to my apartment? I'll be happy to fix you some lunch."

"Th-that would be nice." *Just because her last name is Parker, it doesn't mean she'll know Robert…or his family.* "Thank you." She forced a smile. "In the meantime, don't rob anything."

Greta pointed at her. "I won't if you won't."

Chapter Four

❋

GRETA WENT OUT IN the hallway to report back to the Silver Sleuths.

"So, here's the deal. She's ready to confide in me. She's agreed to come to my apartment at one o'clock for lunch."

"Okay, good," Sue said. "I can bring my peanut potato salad."

Opal and Greta exchanged horrified glances. Nobody liked Sue's signature dish. It was something she'd invented, and she thought everybody loved it. Not even Moonshine would eat that stuff.

"I don't want to overwhelm her right off the bat." Greta chose her words carefully. "Why don't I have this lunch with her, and then you guys can come over right afterward for the debriefing?"

"Debriefing? Really? Are we the CIA now?" Sue scoffed. "You just want her to yourself."

"I believe Greta has an excellent point," Opal said. "If we gang up on her, she'll likely clam up. This might be our best chance to find out what she's really doing here in Kinsey Falls."

"Fine." Sue tapped her wrist with two fingers as if she were wearing a watch. "But at two o'clock on the dot, we'll be at your apartment for all the details."

Opal and Gilda nodded.

Gilda picked up Moonshine and kissed the top of his head. "We'll be there with bells on! Well, not with bells…Moonshine doesn't like bells…but we'll be there."

As she walked up the steps to the second level, Greta wondered what to prepare. She wanted the meal to be impressive, so Joanne would feel that Greta was competent. Not competent enough to rob a bank—Greta wasn't looking to be an accessory but rather an intercessor…intervener? Stopper. That's it. She was going to be a bank robbery *stopper*, not a participant. But if Joanne saw that Greta could cook, it would lend some credence to her bake sale idea.

Also, she wanted the girl to feel at home. She felt sorry for the poor thing. Her daddy was in a nursing home, and she was so desperate for money that she was considering robbing a bank. Maybe…they didn't know for sure…but bank robbery seemed to be the Silver Sleuths' best guess.

When she got to her apartment, she hurried into the kitchen to see what she had. Although the kitchen was small, Greta knew how to organize it for maximum efficiency. She enjoyed cooking and always kept plenty of food on hand.

She had yeast, so she could make rolls. And she had a devil's food cake mix. She'd make the rolls and then, while they were rising, make the cake. She could easily doctor the mix using buttermilk, cocoa, and vanilla, and she'd make her own chocolate buttercream. In the freezer, she had a chicken she could quickly defrost in the microwave. Everything was coming together nicely.

* * *

Joanne wiped her damp palms down the sides of her jeans before she tapped on Greta's door.

"Coming!" came the chipper voice from inside the apartment.

She took a deep breath in through her nose and out through her mouth. And another.

How should she start this conversation? Are you related to Robert Parker? He might be my father. No, no, no. That sounded stupid. She didn't want to come across as stupid...or needy...

"Hidey-ho!" Greta said, as she flung open the door. "Welcome to Casa Greta."

Joanne smiled. "Thank you. Whatever you've been cooking smells wonderful. I hope you didn't go to too much trouble on my account."

"No trouble whatsoever." Greta ushered her guest inside and closed the door. "You should see what I can throw together for a bake sale. Bake sales are excellent fundraisers, you know. So many people are on the go these days that they don't stop and take the time to bake things themselves."

"You're right. I imagine you could earn a lot of money with a bake sale."

"Oh, yes. And it beats robbing a bank all to pieces." Greta laughed, but it sounded forced to Joanne.

This woman is really hung up on robbing a bank. Is she hurting for money? Should I offer to pay for lunch? No...that might be insulting.

"Do you have bake sales often?" she asked instead.

"Whenever a good cause arises." Greta leaned toward her. "Do you know of any good causes? Like...you know...helping someone out with medical expenses or something of that nature?"

"Do you have a lot of medical expenses?"

"Me? No, darlin', I'm fit as a Stravinsky fiddle."

"Stradivarius?"

"Bless you!" Greta took Joanne's arm and led her into the kitchen. "I hope I've got something you like. I wasn't sure what to fix."

"This all looks wonderful." Joanne realized she could quickly make a pig of herself at Greta's table, but the main thing was to ask her about Robert Parker. She just needed a polite way to ask. "Greta, your family must love to come to your house for dinners."

"Oh, I don't have any family left…but my friends love it when I cook for them. And, you know, I'm giving lessons to Justin and Kelsey…although Justin doesn't know about Kelsey's lessons, so don't mention it."

"I won't."

After asking what Joanne would like, Greta poured the drinks and they both sat at the table. Joanne helped herself to chicken, mashed potatoes, green beans, and a roll. They ate in silence for a couple of minutes. Joanne's first attempt to ask about Robert Parker had failed, and Greta appeared to have something on her mind as well.

"Everything is delicious, Ms. Parker…Greta. Um…if you don't mind my saying so, you look like something might be troubling you."

Greta sighed and forced a tight smile. "Frankly, I'm worried about you."

"About me?"

"Yes. Justin was here making crepes this morning, and he told me about your dad."

Joanne lowered her gaze. "Having to move him into long-term care has been a terrible blow."

Greta reached over and patted Joanne's hand. "If you're having trouble making ends meet, some of my friends and I are willing to help you any way we can. That's why I told you about the bake sale."

Tears burned the backs of Joanne's eyes. "Thank you, but I'm fine…financially. Emotionally, well, that's another story." *Time to bite the bullet.* "I actually came here to Kinsey Falls to find my birth parents." She swallowed. "Do you know a Robert Parker?"

* * *

Greta covered her mouth with both hands. "You're mine," she whispered. "You're my…Robert's daughter…you're my granddaughter." She got up so forcefully that her chair fell back against the stove. "*My granddaughter!*" She held out her arms, tears streaming down her face.

Joanne was crying now too, and she slowly stood.

Greta threw her arms around the child—her grandchild—and embraced her. Then she pulled back. "Oh, darlin', let me look at you." Her eyes drank in every detail. "You look like your mother."

"But...I haven't told you who my mother is."

"It has to be Carla. Carla Crockett."

Joanne's jaw dropped. "How did you know?"

"I'm telling you—you look just like she did when she was young. She and your father were so much in love. They were going to be married."

This statement brought fresh tears, and Greta hugged Joanne again.

"I know about the car accident," Joanne said quietly.

Greta merely nodded. "He'd have been so proud of you. So happy." She finally let go of Joanne, righted her chair, and sat back down. "I'm afraid my legs will give way if I don't sit down."

"Me too." Joanne sank onto her chair and took a drink of her tea.

"And here we were afraid you were going to try to rob Kinsey Falls Bank." Greta laughed.

Joanne shook her head. "Why would you think that?"

"It's...it's a long story. When we heard about your..." *Her dad...but he's not her dad—Robert is.* "Well, I want to meet your family. I want to thank them for taking such good care of you. And, Joanne, I want you to know that if I'd known about you, I'd have been there for you."

"Thank you." She smiled slightly. "My maternal grandparents didn't feel the same way."

"I can't imagine why Carla wouldn't have let me know," Greta said. "We were close. She was going to be my daughter-in-law. I mean, they weren't officially engaged yet, but—"

"Carla died."

Greta raised a trembling hand to her chest. "Oh, no. I'm so sorry."

"She suffered an ischemic stroke caused by a blood clot."

"I'm sorry." Greta didn't mean to repeat herself, but she didn't know what else to say. There were a million questions floating around in her mind.

"Um…" Joanne cleared her throat. "I don't know for sure that Robert is my dad."

"Well, honey, of course, he is."

"A woman who had been friends with my mom told me it could've been someone else…someone Carla worked for after…after Robert's accident."

Greta shook her head. "No. That's not possible."

"I hope you're right. Would you…" She reached over and took Greta's hand. "Would you submit your DNA for a paternity test?"

"Of course! Just tell me where and when."

Joanne smiled. "We have some home test kits at the pharmacy. I can bring one by tomorrow, if that's okay."

"That'll be fine. That will be absolutely fine." Greta took a steadying breath. "A granddaughter. I have a granddaughter. A smart, beautiful granddaughter."

* * *

Joanne took the elevator back to the lower level and still had to run to make it back to work on time. Still, she might've found what she was looking for when she arrived in Kinsey Falls—a connection.

It was after Joanne's father, John—the wonderful man who'd raised her—had gone to live in the assisted care facility that she'd decided to try to locate her biological parents. John and his wife Marie had been the most wonderful parents Joanne could have ever asked for. But now, Marie was gone—a victim of pancreatic cancer—and, thanks to the dementia, John was a stranger…even to himself. Joanne was alone.

But maybe not anymore. She might have a grandmother. An eccentric grandmother, but a sweet one.

And Greta could tell Joanne what she could recall about Carla. When Joanne had visited Carla's family, they hadn't been welcoming. They'd basically told her that she was a painful reminder of the daughter they'd lost and had made it clear they had no desire to see her again.

She smiled to herself. Greta couldn't have been more different from the Crocketts. She'd invited Joanne to come back after work to get some of the cake to take home. Joanne had declined. She wanted some time alone to process everything. From what Ms. Hazelton had told her, Robert might not be her biological father. She'd told Greta she'd give her a call tomorrow.

She put a paternity test behind the counter, so she could buy it before leaving work. Thanks to modern technology, they should know soon enough whether or not they were related.

Chapter Five

❀

As soon as Joanne left, Greta called Millie.

"Hi. Can you come over?"

"Greta, you're out of breath. Is something wrong?"

"No…I just can't leave because the Silver Sleuths are supposed to be here at two, and I have something I'm dying to tell you."

Greta's doorbell rang.

"That's them," she told Millie. "Just come on over, okay?"

"I'll be right there."

Greta opened the door to Opal, Sue, Gilda, and Moonshine. Millie walked out into the hall and fell in behind them as they filed into Greta's living room.

The Silver Sleuths knew Millie and greeted her warmly. Except Sue. Sue was a little icy, but she did say hello. Greta asked if anyone would like anything to eat or drink.

"No," Sue said. "We just want to know what you've found out about Joanne Faraday."

"Let's sit down." Greta sat on the sofa, looked at Millie, and patted the cushion next to her.

Millie sat beside Greta and patted her hand. "You look pale."

Greta looked up at the ceiling and blinked back tears. "She's...my...granddaughter."

That brought on a reaction from everyone in the room. Even Moonshine let out a bark or two. Once they'd calmed down, Greta explained that Joanne had come to Kinsey Falls looking for her biological parents. She'd tracked down her mother—Carla Crockett.

"Carla? Isn't that the girl Robert dated all through high school?" Millie asked.

Greta nodded.

"And she told you Robert is her father?" Gilda clasped her hands together.

"No... I mean, she doesn't know for sure." Greta frowned. "She talked with some so-called friend of Carla's online who told her that her dad might be some guy Carla met after Robert died. But that's ridiculous. She *has* to be Robert's daughter."

Opal raised her eyebrows and inclined her head.

"You'd better be careful, Greta," Sue cautioned. "You know good and well that Joanne has just put her father in a long-term care facility, and those things cost a lot of money. She might just be looking for somebody to help her out financially."

Greta lifted her chin. "Well, I don't believe that."

"Just this morning, you were convinced the girl was going to rob a bank. Now you believe she's your granddaughter." Sue shrugged. "I'm just telling you not to let your guard down."

"I know...and I appreciate that. But we're going to do a DNA test to prove that Joanne is my granddaughter."

"How?" Opal asked.

"I'm not sure, but Joanne works in the pharmacy so I'm sure she knows all about these things."

"I think it's simply wonderful," Gilda said. "Finding a long-lost relative is so much better than taking down a bank robber." She shook her head. "I wasn't sure we were up to that task."

Millie squeezed Greta's hand. "What time will Steve be here?"

Greta let out her breath. "Soon."

Opal stood. "We'll let you get ready then."

"Yes." Sue patted her forefingers below her eyes. "You'll want to put some teabags or something on your eyes before you fix your makeup. You're a little puffy."

"Thanks." Greta nodded. "I'll do that."

"Keep us posted!" Gilda hugged Greta. "Maybe we could throw you a shower!"

"A shower?" Sue rolled her eyes. "She's not having a baby."

Gilda's face fell. "In a way, she might be. We could at least have a party."

Opal patted Gilda's shoulder. "If it turns out that Greta really is Joanne's grandmother, we will have a party. And, Gilda, you can plan it."

Gilda beamed, first at Opal and then at Greta. "It'll be fun."

When the Silver Sleuths had left, Greta and Millie sat back down on the sofa.

"Thanks for that," Greta said.

"I could tell you were ready for them to leave."

"I was." She smiled. "They mean well, but…"

"I know."

Greta leaned back against the sofa cushions, glad that Millie *did* know and that there wasn't any awkward silence between them.

"Can I get you anything?" Millie asked.

"No." She lolled her head to the left to look at her best friend. "Do you think it's possible? Could I really have a piece of Robert back after all these years without him?"

"I think it's possible." She got up and retrieved the box of tissues that was on Greta's kitchen counter. She took two and handed the box to Greta before sitting back down. "But even Joanne said her biological father could be someone else."

"I know." Greta took a tissue and dabbed at her eyes. "Was Sue right—am I puffy?"

"Tea bags wouldn't hurt."

"Guess we'd better have a cup of tea then."

Millie stood. "I'll put the kettle on."

"Thanks."

"For what? Coming in and acting like I own the place?" Millie laughed.

"Well, that…and for not telling me not to get my hopes up."

* * *

After work, Joanne went to Nothin' But Knit, hoping that a few minutes in the knitting room would help her to unwind. The shop wasn't going to be open for much longer, but Joanne wanted to knit. Even more than that, she wanted to talk with Jade.

"Hi, Jade," she said upon walking into the shop.

Mocha, Jade's seal-point Himalayan, was curled up on the bench near the window. He raised his head, yawned, and watched her disinterestedly.

"Hey, Joanne. Did you just get off work?"

"Yeah. I know you close soon, but I'd like to work on my scarf."

"Sure. Since we're closed tomorrow, would you like to take it home with you?" Jade asked.

Joanne shook her head. "No, thanks. I'm not that ambitious yet."

Jade chuckled. "Chicken."

"I just don't want to tear it up." She followed Jade into the knitting room, glad to see that no one else was using it at the moment. "You seem to know Greta Parker pretty well."

"Yeah. Greta has been my grandmother's best friend for as long as I remember."

"Did…did you…ever hear her talk about her son?"

Jade frowned. "Where's this coming from?"

Joanne looked beyond Jade's shoulder to make sure no one was coming into the room. "There's a chance he…he might be…my birth father."

"Oh, wow! That's great!" Jade bit her lip. "I mean, it *is* great…isn't it?"

"Y-yes. I mean…it's all so new. You know? I…I came to Kinsey Falls to find my birth parents." She lifted and dropped one shoulder. "I found my mom."

"Come on. Forget the knitting, and let's sit down." Jade led her over to the knitting table and pulled out a chair.

Joanne perched on the edge of the chair. "I don't mean to lay all this on you. I just…"

Jade put her hand on Joanne's shoulder. "You just need someone to talk it over with. So, let's talk. Or, rather, you talk; I'll listen."

So, Joanne told Jade about finding her mother, learning that her mother was deceased, and then realizing that her maternal grandparents wanted nothing to do with her.

"Now I've found someone who might be my paternal grandmother," Joanne said, "and she's thrilled."

"But you're not sure."

"I think it would be wonderful if it turned out to be true, but Greta is so excited. What if it turns out that I'm *not* her son's child?"

"Greta knows that's a possibility, right?"

Joanne nodded.

"Then you can't help it if you're not," Jade said. "Do you know who the other possibility is?"

"I do. A man named Winston Wallace."

"The attorney?" Jade turned down the corners of her mouth. "He had a stellar reputation in Kinsey Falls."

"*Had?*" She sighed. "He's dead too? Why is it too much to ask that I could find a living parent?"

"I'm sorry."

"It's okay. I just wanted to make a connection…you know? My mom—the woman who adopted me, I mean—is dead, and my dad is suffering from dementia." Her shoulders slumped. "I hoped to…to…"

"To find another family member?" Jade asked gently.

"Yeah."

"Well…hopefully…you have. If Greta is your grandmother, then she'll stick to you like glue."

* * *

While lying on the sofa with teabags on her eyes, Greta phoned Steve.

"Hello, beautiful," he answered.

"How'd you know it was me?"

"Your pretty face comes up on my phone whenever you call."

"Huh."

"You aren't calling to cancel on me, are you?" Steve asked.

"No. I'm calling to ask you if we can stop by my storage unit on the way to the restaurant."

"Sure. I'll come over a little earlier than I'd anticipated so we won't be late for our reservation."

"Thanks, darlin'."

"What's so urgent?" he asked.

"I…I might…have a granddaughter."

"Really? How are you just now finding that out?"

Greta told him how she'd met Joanne, believed she was up to something underhanded, and then learned that there was a possibility the young woman was her granddaughter.

"Even if she isn't," Greta said, "I have photos of her mother with Robert that I'm sure Joanne would like to see. Carla's parents weren't friendly with Joanne, and the poor girl has so many questions. I hope I can help her know her mother just a teensy bit."

"You're an amazing woman. You know that?"

"That's what my handsome fella tells me."

Steve laughed.

"Gotta go, love," Greta said. "I have a hot date I have to get ready for."

* * *

44

Joanne was searching online to see what she could learn about Winston Wallace.

Man! Am I cursed or something? I try to find my biological parents, and they're all dead.

Pushing her depressing thoughts aside, she continued reading the bio she'd found and learned that Winston Wallace, Esquire, was a founding member of the firm Wallace, Pembroke, and Allen.

Wait…isn't that the name of Andrew's firm?

She picked up her phone. They had exchanged numbers. He wouldn't have given her his number had he not wanted her to call…right?

She sighed. By being so forward, she very well might chase him off. But, if that was the case, he wasn't interested in her anyway. Besides, Kelsey said he was uber focused on his career. Joanne decided that calling Andrew to find out if Winston Wallace was her father was a risk she had to take.

"Hi, Joanne." Andrew's greeting was simple and sounded pleasant enough. She'd expected him to add "what's up" or "how are you," but he didn't.

She swallowed. "I hope this isn't a bad time."

"Not really. I'm working on a contract that must be sent out tomorrow, but I was needing a break."

"I'm calling to ask you about Winston Wallace…but we can talk later. I don't want to interrupt your work."

"Winston Wallace? He was one of our firm's founders. They kept his name to honor his legacy." He paused. "Have you eaten?"

"No…but I was getting ready to make some spaghetti, if you're interested."

"I'm definitely interested—I love pasta. Would you mind if I come over?"

"Not at all," Joanne said. "Should I call and invite Kelsey?"

"Nah, I think she's doing something with Justin this evening."

"All right. I'll look forward to seeing you soon."

After ending the call, Joanne hurried to check her hair and makeup, put on a spritz of perfume, and then started making dinner.

When Andrew arrived, he closed his eyes and relished the delicious aromas. "Your apartment smells heavenly. Did you make garlic bread, too?"

"I heated up garlic bread that I bought at the café."

"I can hardly wait," he said.

Joanne laughed and led him into the kitchen. "It's only right that I should feed you. I'm the one asking for information."

"Why do you want to know about Mr. Wallace?"

"Someone who knew my mother told me she used to work for him." Joanne took two glasses from the cabinet. "Would you like tea, water, lemonade, soda?"

"Lemonade, please."

She filled one glass with lemonade and the other with tea. She placed the glasses on the table and invited Andrew to take a seat and dig in.

He waited until she was seated before he began ladling spaghetti onto his plate. "So…you're…what? Researching the places your mom used to work?"

"Something like that. I'm trying to learn more about her. My mom died when I was a child."

"Oh. I'm sorry."

"But, Mr. Wallace is dead, and I doubt anyone left at the firm would remember her." Joanne filled her plate.

"I wouldn't be too sure," Andrew said. "Mr. Wallace has only been dead for about three years. His secretary Margaret, whom the firm kept on as receptionist, is still there. She's been with the company for about thirty-five years."

"Wow…that's a long time."

He chuckled. "Yeah. She's sixty-eight. I think Mr. Wallace was the first person to give her a job out of secretarial school." He gestured toward the plate with his fork. "I'm so happy that Greta is teaching

Kelsey to cook. My poor sister has no talent whatsoever in the kitchen."

"I might have to get some lessons myself." She sipped her tea.

"Hardly. This is delicious."

"Do you think it would be possible for me to buy Margaret lunch one day this coming week and ask her if she remembers my mother?" Joanne asked.

"I'll ask her. If anyone at the firm would remember Carla, it would be Margaret—she remembers everybody."

Chapter Six

❀

"THEY MIGHT NOT COME," Greta said, as Steve looked at his watch for about the fifteenth time in as many minutes.

"It would suit me fine if Mitch doesn't show up, but Terri had better be here." He took out his phone. "I'm going to text her to see where they're at."

"Wait, Steve. I see them." Greta waved to the couple weaving through the dining room to get to their table. Mitch nodded and spoke to a few people on the way over.

"So sorry," he said, sliding into the booth beside Greta. "Everywhere I go, I'm accosted by people who've seen me on the news. They feel a kinship with me because they see me every day, I suppose." He kissed Greta's cheek. "You look lovely."

"Thank you," she said, hoping Mitch missed Steve's eyeroll at the remark about being accosted. As Steve liked to say, Mitch loved him some Mitch. But as long as he loved Terri, too, Greta didn't have a problem with him.

Terri sat beside Steve. "What's wrong, Grumpy Gus?"

"I'm hungry...and you've held us up for fifteen minutes."

"That's entirely my fault," Mitch said. "On our way here, we came upon an accident."

"We pulled over to the side of the road, and Mitch hopped out of the car to see if he could help out," Terri said.

"How nice." Greta raised her eyebrows at Steve in what she hoped would convey, See? He did something heroic. "I didn't realize you had EMT training."

"I don't." Mitch waved away Greta's praise with the flick of his wrist. "I stopped to see if the accident was newsworthy. I shouldn't have bothered—just a fender bender between two nobodies."

"Um...well...thank goodness for that," Greta said.

Steve raised his glass and inclined his head in a gesture that emphatically said, What've I been telling you?

"If it had been a major accident, Mitch would've certainly gotten the story," Terri said.

"Not all of us have it easy like you, my sweet," Mitch said. "I'd like a cushy job where I didn't have to do anything more difficult than to knit all day."

Steve's face hardened.

Greta hurried to fill the silence before Steve beat her to it. "I don't think you can really know what all goes into running a business until you've done it. I admire Terri so much for having the temerity to open her own shop right out of college."

"Thank you, Greta. Jade and I did it together, though. It wasn't all me."

"Still, it took a lot of courage for the two of you to dive into that venture and make a success of it." Greta decided to take this opportunity to show off her new knowledge. "Maybe you could do a TED Talk for other young entrepreneur-wannabes."

* * *

Andrew insisted on helping Joanne clean up.

"I'm serious—next time, dinner is one me. But I can't promise it'll be this good," he said.

When the kitchen was presentable once again, Joanne asked Andrew if he'd like to have some coffee in the living room.

Any excuse to have him linger just a while longer.

"I'd love some coffee, thanks." Andrew went into the living room and sat on the sofa.

Joanne took that as a good sign as she prepared the coffee tray. Had he not wanted to sit near her, he would've taken the armchair.

She brought the tray into the living room and placed it on the low wooden coffee table.

"Did you always want to be an attorney?" she asked, as she sat down beside him.

"No." He poured them each a cup of coffee. "I wanted to be the Green Lantern, but I never could find the ring." He shrugged. "I mean, Mom got me several over the years, but none of them actually worked."

She laughed. "That's too bad."

He added creamer and sugar to his cup. "So, what about you? Did you always dream of working in pharmaceuticals?"

"I'd never even considered it, and yet, that's where I wound up. I enjoy it though." She sipped her black coffee. "Was becoming a lawyer your way of providing truth, justice, and the American way in a more conventional manner?"

Andrew raised his eyebrows. "Don't you know your superheroes? Truth, justice, and the American way is Superman's thing. The Green Lantern Corps preserve order in the entire galaxy."

"I'm so sorry. I had no idea."

"Had no idea?" He sat his coffee cup back on the tray. "I think I might need to leave if you don't know any more than *that* about superheroes. Who did you look up to while you were growing up?"

"The Powerpuff Girls."

He slapped his hand to his forehead. "You need an education about superheroes. To learn about superheroes is what you need.

Learning about superheroes is what you must do!"

Joanne started laughing. He was imitating one of the show's villains who repeated everything ad nauseum.

"You watched that show too!" she cried, when she could catch her breath.

"I had to watch it with Kelsey. We had to take turns choosing our programs."

"You have to admit, though, it was good."

He waffled his hand back and forth. "Are you busy tomorrow night?"

"Not that I know of. Why?"

"I'm bringing over a pizza and some DVDs," he said. "Time for your education to begin."

* * *

The waitress brought the bill and placed it onto the table. Mitch excused himself to go to the men's room. Steve picked up the black bill holder and opened it. He casually perused the tab before taking his wallet from his back pocket. He placed a credit card into the plastic slot, placed the bill holder upright on the edge of the table and sat back.

"Thank you for dinner," Greta said. "It was wonderful."

"Yes, Uncle Steve. Thank you."

"You're both welcome," he said.

The waitress picked up the folder and said she'd be right back.

Greta smiled at Terri. "Would you and Mitch like to go dancing with us at the Elks Lodge now?"

"No, thank you," Terri said. "Even though Nothin' But Knit is closed tomorrow, Mitch still has to be at the television station early."

Mitch came back just in time to hear Terri's response. "That's right," he said, sliding back into the booth. "It must be nice to get to sleep in tomorrow."

"It will be." Terri smiled over at Mitch.

Greta knew good and well that Terri never slept in on her day off. First, she'd walk on the indoor track, and then she'd attend Kelsey's early yoga class. But if Terri wanted to let Mitch think she was a laze-about, so be it.

The waitress returned with the check holder and handed it to Steve. When she'd left, he added a tip, tallied up the bill, and signed the receipt.

"We appreciate your buying us dinner, Uncle Steve," Mitch said. "Terri and I will have to return the favor sometime." He nodded at Terri. "Ready?"

"Sure." She kissed Steve's cheek. "Thanks again, Uncle Steve."

"It was Greta's idea," he said.

Terri looked across the table at Greta. "Thank you. I enjoyed spending time with the two of you."

"We enjoyed it, too, darlin'."

As Greta and Steve left the restaurant, Steve mumbled, "I don't know what she sees in that jerk."

Greta laughed. "Terri is probably saying the same thing to Mitch about me."

Steve snorted. "That's rich. I'll tell you what I see in you. You're beautiful, thoughtful, loving…and sexy as heck!"

Greta grinned all the way to the Elks Lodge.

Chapter Seven

GRETA WAS BENT OVER tying her walking shoes when she heard her doorbell. She thought maybe Millie had decided to go walking with her.

"Coming!" She hurried to open the door. "Terri…this is a nice surprise."

Terri, her blonde hair up in a ponytail and her face flushed and damp with perspiration, held out a liter bottle of ruby-red liquid. "Kelsey sent you some iced hibiscus tea."

"Thank you." Greta took the plastic bottle and jerked her head. "Would you like to come in? You look exhausted."

"Um…I guess I can for a minute. I need to get home and shower, though. I just finished Kelsey's yoga class."

"That young 'un amazes me." Greta shook her head. "She does that dance and yoga stuff all day long." She took the bottle into the kitchen. "Would you like some of this before I put it away?"

"No, thanks. But I would love a glass of water."

Greta put the tea in the fridge and took out a bottle of water for Terri.

"Thank you." Terri nodded at Greta's shoes. "Am I keeping you from walking?"

"Nah, I'll go when we're finished visiting. That's one of the perks of living in a temperature-controlled environment."

"Yeah."

"Would you like to sit down?" Greta asked.

"No, I can't stay. I just wanted to say that I'm sorry I haven't been supportive of you and Uncle Steve." She cleared her throat. "When I first heard you guys were dating, I didn't think you had much in common and…" She shrugged. "Frankly, it's hard for me to see Uncle Steve with someone besides Aunt Barbara."

"I understand."

"But after seeing the two of you together last night," Terri continued, "I realized how good you are for each other. I believe you make him happy…and vice versa."

"I'm glad you feel that way. My only concern about dating Steve has been that it appeared to have cost me your friendship."

"I'm sorry. I hope you'll forgive me because I'm fortunate to have you in my life. And Uncle Steve is too."

* * *

Typical Monday. It was one of the busiest days for a pharmacy technician. Doctors returning to their offices after the weekend found stacks of messages from patients who'd ran out of their meds over the weekend…and that was in addition to patients being seen and prescribed medications on Monday morning. On top of the volume of work was the aggravation of having customers standing in front of you asking why you haven't yet filled the prescription they handed you ten minutes ago.

"Joanne Faraday, phone call on line one."

Joanne pointed up at the ceiling as if God—and not the store intercom—had summoned her. "I have to take this. Excuse me."

The woman awaiting her prescription sniffed. "Maybe I should just take my business elsewhere."

Maybe you should. "I'll be right back with you. In the meantime, another tech is working on your prescription."

Joanne stepped into the office and answered the call. "This is Joanne Faraday. How may I help you?"

"Good morning. This is Andrew. I spoke with Margaret, and she'd love to have lunch with you. She says she remembers your mother well."

"That's fantastic! When does she want to meet?"

"She said she could do it today or tomorrow."

With her free hand, Joanne pinched the bridge of her nose. Tomorrow would be better from a work point of view, but she was anxious to see what Margaret had to say. For once, Joanne wouldn't be grabbing a quick snack in the breakroom on a Monday rather than taking her lunch break.

"Tell her I'll see her today. When and where?"

After Andrew gave her the details, Joanne asked if he'd be joining them.

"I'm afraid not," he said. "I have to put the finishing touches on that contract. But I'm still planning on seeing you this evening. Are we still on for pizza and superhero movies?"

"Of course. That sounds fun."

* * *

Greta was on her second lap around the Community Center's indoor walking track when Millie joined her. Her bestie was the picture of sophisticated elegance unless she was walking. Then, it was strictly sweatpants and t-shirts. Today's t-shirt read: IF YOU THINK **ADULTING** IS HARD, TRY **SENIORING**!

"I love that shirt," Greta said.

"Thanks. I made it at Redbubble. I see all over social media where these kids are posting that they can't adult today or that adulting is hard," Millie said. "I'm not saying it's *not* hard, but I'm with Bette Davis: Old age ain't for sissies."

Greta threw back her head and laughed. "That's great. I need to get one of those."

"I'll order you one."

"I'm surprised you and Jade aren't doing something today," Greta said.

"She and Caleb took his boat out on the lake today."

"You mean that thing with the pedals?"

Millie nodded. "That's the one. They took me out on it one afternoon last week, and that did me. That little raft with the canopy over it didn't strike me as all that substantial, and I'm not as adventurous as I used to be."

"You're plenty adventurous!" Greta took a sip from her water bottle. "Jade is happier now than I've ever seen her."

"She's happier than *I've* ever seen her," Millie said.

"What about Fiona? Is she coming around yet?"

"My daughter and my granddaughter will butt heads until the end of time. Fiona still bugs Jade about having a more secure career and asks her every chance she gets when Caleb is going to finish up his education and get a *real* job."

"Does Jade climb her frame?" Greta asked.

"Nope. Jade just tells her mother to go to grass."

Both women laughed.

"She got that expression from you, you know," Greta said. "I've heard you say it a thousand times."

"Well, it's a good one. How was your double date last night?"

"It went well. Thank you for that idea. As a matter of fact, Terri even came by this morning to apologize for being snotty about my relationship with Steve. She said it was hard seeing him with anyone except her aunt but that she feels Steve and I are good for each other."

"I'm glad. I guess it's especially hard on Terri to see Steve enjoying himself so much with Ms. Life-of-the-Party Parker since her aunt is Woe-is-Me-Barbara." Millie grinned.

"I reckon. But it's Barbara's own fault! She's the one who left Steve for that tennis player when their girls were young. And, then, Mr. My-Racket-or-Yours dumped her because he wanted a mistress, not a wife and step-children!" She huffed. "Served her right. Oh! I made a pun! See what I did there?"

Millie laughed and shook her head. "I do. But I wouldn't lob that one over the net at Terri. I kinda doubt she'd appreciate it."

* * *

Joanne arrived at the restaurant and looked around for Margaret. Andrew had said she'd have a large, yellow purse sitting on the table.

There it was—a sunny yellow pocketbook with a polka-dot scarf tied around the handle. She lifted a hand and waved, and Margaret— an older woman with slate-gray curls hugging her scalp—returned the greeting. As Joanne approached the table, Margaret adjusted her thick, black-rimmed glasses as if to get a closer look.

Joanne ran her palms down the sides of her black pants. "Are you Margaret?"

"I sure am. And you have to be Joanne. You look so much like your momma I feel like I've stepped back in time." She took the purse off the table and hung it on her chair. "Please have a seat."

"Thank you." Joanne pulled out a chair and sat.

"How do you know Andrew?" Margaret asked.

"His sister Kelsey introduced us."

"Well, it's a good thing most sisters are matchmakers." She winked.

Joanne started to tell Margaret the relationship wasn't like that…that she and Andrew had only just met…but she decided not to waste valuable time on something inconsequential to the meeting. She was too eager to get the information she came for.

The waitress approached, and the women ordered their drinks.

"I'm ready to order my meal as well," Joanne said. "I mean, if that's all right."

"It's perfectly fine," said the waitress.

Both Joanne and Margaret ordered the chef's salad.

"Andrew said you might remember my mother," Joanne said, as the waitress walked away. "I'm so glad you do."

"I remember Carla well," Margaret said. "She came to work for Mr. Wallace right out of high school. She was such a beautiful and tragic young woman." She gave a slight chuckle. "You'll have to forgive me—I have the soul of a poet...even dabble a little bit."

"But why did you see my mom as tragic?"

"Because she'd so recently lost the young man she'd hoped to marry. Did you know about that?"

"Oh, yes...Robert Parker."

Margaret nodded gravely. "I believe tragedy is what brought Carla and Mr. Wallace together. Carla had lost her boyfriend, and Mr. and Mrs. Wallace had just miscarried a baby."

"So, it was true? My mother and Mr. Wallace had an affair?"

"Shh." Margaret put a finger to her lips. "Very few people knew. In fact, I wouldn't have said anything had I not believed you already knew Mr. Wallace was your father."

Chapter Eight

"ALL-RIGHTY," GRETA SAID, as she handed Kelsey an apron. "Today we're making chicken fried steak with gravy."

"Have you taught Justin how to make this?" Kelsey asked, slipping the Marilyn apron over her head and tying it at her back.

Greta was teaching both Justin and Kelsey how to cook. Kelsey knew about Justin's cooking lessons. Justin didn't know about Kelsey's. The girl was hoping to impress him without letting him know they had the same teacher. In fact, Kelsey didn't want Justin to know she had *any* teacher.

"No. I've taught him how to grill a steak but not to make steak like this."

"Good. He's coming over tonight, and I want him to think I just whipped this up." Kelsey beamed at Greta.

Greta patted Kelsey's arm. She was such a beautiful girl—not much more than a child...but, then again, neither was Justin. "Darlin', are you sure you and Justin are headed in the same direction?"

Kelsey's eyes widened. "Has he said something to you? Is he talking to someone else?"

"No, it's not that. It's just that the boy seems to be dragging his feet as far as a relationship goes."

"Oh, that." Kelsey waved away Greta's concern with a flick of her wrist. "He's like Andrew, my brother. They both want to be firmly established in their businesses before they pursue a serious relationship with anyone. You know, they're trying to keep their priorities in order."

"Honey, love usually don't give a gnat's hair for priorities."

"I know, but I can wait. Justin is worth it."

"Well, I love both of you dearly, and I don't want to see either of you get your feelings hurt."

"That makes two of us," Kelsey said. "So...how do we fix this steak?"

Greta took the hint. "First, we need to get everything ready to bread our steak. We want to have kind of an assembly line. We'll dredge the steak through the milk and egg, and then coat both sides in the flour mixture."

Kelsey was doing a slow nod.

Greta gave her a demonstration.

"You do one piece at a time?" Kelsey asked.

"That's right. Give it a go."

Kelsey dutifully and painstakingly did what Greta had shown her.

"Good job! Now put that one on the plate beside the one I did, and when we get them all done, we'll put them in the skillet."

As they were taking turns breading the steaks, Greta said, "I might be a grandmother."

"That's so exciting!"

Greta watched as Kelsey's face registered first excitement and then confusion. Before she could ask, Greta explained the situation with Joanne.

Kelsey smiled. "I met on Joanne Saturday. She and I, Justin, and Andrew went to play mini-golf."

"That's wonderful. I'm so glad she met you. She's relatively new to Kinsey Falls, and I was afraid she might be having trouble making friends."

"Ah, you know me. I talk to everybody. And I believe she and Andrew really hit it off, but I did warn her not to fall for him because of the work thing."

"Yeah, that was probably good advice," Greta said, thinking it was ironic how some people could look directly into a mirror and not recognize themselves.

* * *

Greta called Joanne that afternoon. "Hidey-ho! I hate to bother you, but I have some photos of your mom and dad that I thought you might like to see."

Joanne asked if it would be all right if she came on over.

"Perfectly all right. Even though Steve took home some of that chocolate cake last night, and I gave some to Millie, Kelsey, and Justin, I still have too much of it hanging around here. If you don't come over, I might eat it all myself and be as big as a house."

"Hardly," Joanne said with a laugh.

When Joanne arrived, Greta was glad to see that she'd brought the paternity test kit.

"We might want to do that DNA swab before we eat this devil's food cake," she told Joanne, nodding toward the table where there were two large pieces of cake and a two mugs of coffee waiting.

"Good idea."

They did their cheek swabs, and Joanne put everything into the envelope.

"I'll send this off tomorrow," she said.

Greta held up her crossed fingers.

"Now...about that cake." She moved over to the coffee table where Greta had also put out some photo albums and some loose photographs.

61

Plucking one off the top of a stack, Greta said, "I wanted to show you this one first. It's your mom and dad…well, Robert…at a high school dance. Wasn't she beautiful? And look how much you favor her."

The young woman in the photograph was a stranger to Joanne, but, yes, she could see a resemblance. Their hair was the same golden blonde, eyes the same brown, and Carla even had one dimple on the left side of her cheek just like Joanne did.

Robert had light brown hair, blue eyes, and an impish grin. A glance at Greta showed a face filled with love, pride, pain, and longing as she gazed down at her son's face.

Joanne wondered what Carla and Robert would have looked like had they lived to…well, to grow up. Would either of them have been happy to have a daughter? Would either have welcomed her into her or his life?

Greta patted Joanne's shoulder. "Aren't they gorgeous? So young…happy." She whisked a tissue out of the nearby box and turned away.

"He looks mischievous," Joanne said.

"Oh, he was," Greta said, with a hoot of laughter. "I never knew what he was going to come up with next."

"He's handsome too." Joanne studied the photograph to see if there was anything about Robert that looked vaguely familiar.

Greta appeared to be doing the same thing. "You know, I think you've got his nose."

Joanne nodded. She didn't really see it, but she knew how badly Greta wanted to.

"I brought some of Robert's yearbooks from the storage unit too," Greta said. "I thought you might want to go through them and see what clubs your mom was in…things like that."

"I'd love to. Thank you." Joanne's attention drifted back to the photograph of her mother and the young man who might've been her father. "What were they like? Did you know any of my mom's friends?"

"I didn't really know any of Carla's friends, but I can tell you that they were both smart…they made good grades in school. Robert was athletic and funny and compassionate. Your mother played the piano."

"Really?"

Greta nodded. "She played beautifully. She was very musically inclined."

They talked and ate and looked at photographs for over two hours. At last, Joanne said she needed to get home.

"Take the yearbooks with you," Greta said. "I think you'll have fun looking through them."

"Thank you. For everything. This has been wonderful."

"Yes, it has."

Greta hugged her, and Joanne hugged her back.

* * *

Steve pushed away from Greta's table and patted his stomach. "Woman, you're going to turn me into a Weeble. Remember those toys? Their slogan was *Weebles wobble, but they don't fall down.*"

Greta laughed. "I do remember those. Robert had some, and I enjoyed playing with them more than he did."

"I can just imagine you sitting on the floor playing with toys." He took her hand. "I know you were a wonderful mom."

"Yeah, well, you're just buttering me up, so you can have a big piece of cake."

"I'm stuffed. I honestly can't eat another bite," he said. "Why did you make so much food anyway?"

"Kelsey had a cooking lesson today. We made a lot, so she could invite Justin for supper." She sighed. "I worry about those two…and now that she's told me about Andrew seeing Joanne, I'm worried about Joanne too. I don't want my granddaughter to get her heart broken."

"Sweetheart." Steve raised her hand to his lips and kissed it. "You don't know for sure that Joanne *is* your granddaughter."

"Yes, I do. I don't need a DNA test to tell me anything. Joanne is Robert and Carla's child…and she's my granddaughter. I can feel it in my heart."

"I hope you're right."

Greta jerked her head toward the living room. "Let's go snuggle and see what's on TV."

* * *

Joanne was surprised to see that, along with a large cheese pizza, Andrew had brought three superhero movies.

"Didn't you think one would be enough?" she asked, with a laugh. "After all, we both have work tomorrow."

"I do believe we'll only have time for one tonight, but I couldn't choose. So, we'll start with one—your choice—and leave the other ones for another evening."

She looked at the three DVD cases before plucking one from his fingers. "I vote for the one with the female lead. Let me get the plates and napkins."

"While you do that, I'll put in the movie."

"Sounds great. Would you like soda, iced tea, or water?"

"Water works for me," he said. "I don't need any more caffeine today."

When Joanne returned to the living room with everything they needed, Andrew asked about lunch.

"I meant to stop by Margaret's desk and ask her," Andrew said, "but she was gone before I had the chance."

"It was really nice. You were absolutely right about Margaret—she remembered my mother well."

"I'm glad. Did she regale you with lots of anecdotes?"

"A few." Joanne struggled about whether or not to tell Andrew what Margaret *had* told him about Carla. Although Margaret had told Joanne that few people knew about the affair between Carla and Mr. Wallace, Joanne felt sure Andrew would be discreet. On the other hand, she didn't want Andrew to think she had an ulterior motive for wanting to talk with Margaret or that she wanted anything from Mr. Wallace's family.

Andrew winked at her as he slid a slice of pizza from the box onto the plate.

"Do you need a fork?" she asked.

"Not me. But, if you do, feel free."

She smiled. "I don't need one either. That's why I brought extra napkins."

Joanne desperately hoped the paternity test would show that Robert Parker was her biological father.

* * *

After Andrew left, Joanne made herself a cup of kava tea and sat on the sofa. The movie had been good, and the company had been even better. She really liked Andrew. He was a wonderful guy…and very easy on the eyes.

She raised one index finger to gently trace her lips, remembering the goodnight kiss Andrew had given her. That kiss had been even better than the one in her dream.

Kelsey's warning that her brother refused to get serious about anyone until he felt he was successful in his law practice was a red flag that seemed far off in the distance. It was there, but Joanne could pretend it wasn't. Not that she wanted a serious relationship at this point in her life, either.

Get real, Joanne, that's a lie.

She came to Kinsey Falls because she was so desperate for relationships. With her mother gone and her father battling dementia—and losing—Joanne wanted to find a mom or a dad or a boyfriend or a grandmother or anyone she could call her own.

Once again, she hoped that the paternity results would prove her to be Robert's daughter…Greta's granddaughter. She felt that Greta needed the connection as much as Joanne did.

But what if she *wasn't* Robert's daughter? Should she reach out to Eve Wallace? Margaret had said that, coincidentally enough, Eve was also a resident of the Kinsey Falls Living and Retail Community Center.

No, Joanne decided. She'd wait for the paternity test results. She didn't want to intrude upon Eve Wallace's life if she didn't have to.

Chapter Nine

D URING THEIR WALK ON Tuesday morning, Greta and Millie saw a flurry of activity near one of the vacant buildings.

"Oooh!" Greta raised her fists up under her chin. "I see hardhats and tool belts! Let's investigate."

"Normally, I'd say no to your investigating, but I'm curious too," Millie said.

The women hurried over to the shop and peered inside. The workers had blocked the entrance—or, at least, shown that they didn't want any visitors—with a couple of sawhorses. Greta pushed these aside and strolled on through as if they were saloon doors.

"Greta!" Millie hissed.

"Come on." She motioned for Millie to join her in the shop. "What fine work! Look at those display cases. What's going in here—some kind of food shop?"

"It's a candy shop."

The young man smiling down at Greta looked like that fellow who played Superman.

Being the type of person to say the first thing that sprang to mind, Greta said, "Aren't you handsome? You look like that fellow who played Superman."

He laughed. "My name's Cade."

"Nice to meet you, Cade. I'm Greta, and this is my friend Millie."

Cade shook their hands.

"What are they putting in here?" Millie asked.

"Carson's Confectionery."

"A candy shop." Greta clasped her hands together. "I love candy. What's the owner like?"

"I hear he looks like that fellow who played Superman," Cade said, with a chuckle.

"Oh, it's you!" Greta laughed. "That's wonderful. Looks and talent…you know, I've got a granddaughter about your age."

"Greta!" Millie shook her head. "I'm sorry, Cade. We can dress her up, but we can't take her anywhere."

"How'd you come to be a candy-maker?" Greta asked.

"I learned from the best—my grandfather." Cade led them around the shop, showing them what he was doing. "We don't really need many tables since people usually get candy to go, but I want to have a few bistro tables in case people want to sit and chat over a buckeye or a slab of fudge."

"Some people might want to come and watch you work," Greta said.

Millie elbowed her in the ribs.

"What?" Greta asked her friend. "There's an art to good candy-making." She paused. "Cade, I'd love to learn how to make divinity. How much would you charge to teach me and my friend Kelsey how to make it?"

"I wouldn't charge you a penny," Cade said. "I'd be glad to do it." He took a business card from his shirt pocket and handed it to her. "Just call me to set up a time."

"All right." She smiled. "We'd better let you get back to work. You might want to put up some of that yellow caution tape or something to keep out the looky-loos."

"I'll do that, Greta. Thanks."

As they continued on their walk, Greta noticed Millie looking at her.

"You'd better watch where you're going before you run into something," Greta said.

"What are you up to now? You make the best divinity I've ever put in my mouth."

"Well, it never pays to get the big head. If Cade can teach me a better way, I'll try it."

Millie's eyes narrowed. "Are you matchmaking?"

"Not exactly."

"From what you said to him about having a granddaughter his age, I thought you were trying to fix him up with Joanne; but then you bring up Kelsey." She stopped. "Tell me what you're doing."

Millie had stopped so abruptly that Greta had to go back a couple of steps. "Fine. You know I love Kelsey and Justin, and I think they're a fine couple. They just don't seem to know they're a couple—or, at least, Justin doesn't. Maybe it's time he had a little competition."

"And what if your plan backfires?"

"I told you. I don't have a plan. I'm just stirring the pot a little bit…and the pot needed some sugar. Cade. He's the sugar."

"I get it." Millie shook her head and resumed walking. "Just don't come complaining to me when they all get mad at you."

* * *

At the pharmacy, a tall, thin woman with chestnut-colored hair cut in a stylish bob stood at the consultation window.

Joanne greeted her with a bright smile. "Hi, there. How can I help you?"

"Are you Joanne Faraday?"

"Yes," Joanne said, her smile fading. There was something in the woman's tone that put her on high alert. Had something happened to her dad?

"I'm Eve Wallace. You and I need to talk."

Thoughts raced through Joanne's head at breakneck speed: *What is Eve Wallace doing here? Why does she want to talk with me? Does she know about her husband's affair with my mom? Does she believe—or know—that I'm Winston Wallace's daughter?*

"When do you have a break?" Eve asked.

"I'll be able to take my lunch break in about fifteen minutes."

"All right. Will you meet me in the café?"

Joanne nodded.

"Good. I'll be waiting for you."

Eve turned and walked away. Joanne stared at the woman's retreating back—elegantly draped in a red silk blouse—until a man called out to her.

"I'm sorry," Joanne said, turning to her customer.

"I had to call to you twice," he grumbled. "Instead of wool-gathering, why don't you get me my prescription?"

He gave her his name, and with shaking hands, Joanne rifled through the bags until she found the one containing the man's medicine.

On the one hand, it felt as if hours were passing; and on the other, time seemed to be flying by. And then it was time for Joanne to go talk with Eve Wallace. She left the pharmacy and trudged to the café as if she were walking through molasses.

What would Eve say? This could go really badly...or really well. Only one way to find out.

Although her stomach was fluttering like crazy, Joanne went to the counter and bought a pistachio muffin and an iced tea. It gave her a little extra time to pull herself together before she approached the corner table where Eve sat nursing a cup of coffee.

Joanne's hands were shaking so badly that she spilled a little of her iced tea as she placed it onto the table.

Eve wiped up the spill with her napkin. "There's no need to be nervous, Joanne. I simply want to know what you hope to gain by announcing that Winston is your father."

"I don't know that Mr. Wallace *is* my father." Joanne sat in the chair across from Eve. "Do you?"

"No," Eve said, with a shake of her head. "I thought you at least *believed* Winston to be your biological father."

"I know Margaret seems to think so."

Eve lowered her eyes, telling Joanne she was correct in guessing the source of Eve's information.

Joanne continued, emboldened by the thought that Eve Wallace believed she was out to get something from the family. "I'm currently awaiting the results of a paternity test that I expect will prove that Robert Parker—my mother's high-school sweetheart—is my father."

Eve sipped her coffee, wrinkling her nose in distaste before pushing it away. "It's cold." She cleared her throat. "I'm sorry I was so abrupt with you. A few years ago—before Winston died—a woman came to us and claimed that Winston was the father of her child. The woman had worked at the firm, and I don't know whether my husband had an affair with her or not. I do know that Winston was not the father of her child. This woman was merely in dire financial straits and hoped to get some money out of us."

"And you thought that's what I was after," Joanne said flatly.

"I'm sorry. Once burned, twice shy, you know."

"I don't want anything from anyone except to know who my birth parents are."

"Again, I apologize," Eve said. "But if you're certain this Mr. Parker is your father, why were you talking with Margaret?"

"Because I'm *not* certain...especially since Margaret was convinced that Mr. Wallace was my biological father."

"Yes, well...Margaret often talks when she shouldn't. Still, with

Winston dead, I'm not sure how you could prove paternity."

Joanne lifted and dropped one shoulder. "Actually, Robert is dead too. We're comparing my DNA with that of his mother. If you and Mr. Wallace have children…"

"Absolutely not." Eve shook her head vehemently. "Amber is our only child, and she thought the sun rose and set on her father. I knew better—there had always been whispers of affairs—but Amber never knew. She just found out she's pregnant with her first child, and she's hoping for a boy, so she can name him after her father." Eve blinked back tears. "She lives out of town, but she's coming to visit this weekend. Maybe I could take a few hairs from her brush. Would that work?"

Joanne took a drink of the tea she'd been neglecting.

"I'm sure that's not ideal, but Amber has been really sick," Eve went on. "She'd be devastated if she learned that her father wasn't the man she thought he was."

Joanne was thinking that Amber probably knew more about her father than she was willing to admit, but she didn't want to burst Eve's bubble. Nor did she want to hurt either of the Wallace women.

"Why don't we wait until the results come back from the Parker DNA?" she asked gently. "If Robert Parker is my dad, then you'll have no reason to get Amber's DNA. She'll never have to know."

"Thank you." Eve gave Joanne her phone number and asked her to let her know as soon as possible.

* * *

Greta had a hankering for one of the café's chicken salad croissants for lunch. When she walked in, she spotted Joanne sitting in the corner. There was someone with her, but Greta had to say hello. It would've been impolite not to.

She walked over to the table. "Hidey-ho! I don't want to interrupt. I just wanted to say hello and that I hope you're having a good day."

"Greta, this is Eve Wallace," Joanne said. "Eve, Greta Parker."

"Parker…" Eve smiled slightly. "It's nice to meet you."

"Right back-at-cha." Greta smiled at her granddaughter. "Joanne, you look so pretty in that light blue blouse." She turned back to Eve. "Doesn't Joanne look gorgeous in pastels? They make me look washed out, but Joanne has that warm tone to her skin that makes them pop—just like her mother did."

Eve looked at her watch. "If you'll excuse me, I have an errand to run. Joanne, I'll talk with you soon."

"Would you like to join me?" Joanne asked Greta, as Eve hurried out the door. "I still have plenty of time before my lunch hour is up."

"I'd love to." Greta slid onto the seat vacated by Eve. "What was with the stuffy woman?"

Joanne explained that, according to a woman who worked in Winston Wallace's law firm, Carla had an affair with Mr. Winston. "She believes he could be my father."

"Oh." Greta lowered her head. "I hope not. I realize I'm being selfish, but when you came along, I thought I'd found the one thing I'd never have again—family. Granted, I have some wonderful friends, and I have Steve…but even if Steve and I were to get married, his extended family would be *his* family. You know?"

"I do know. And I feel the same way."

Greta lifted her chin. "You do?"

Joanne nodded. "I really want to be your granddaughter."

"Yeah." Greta brightened. "Because if you're not, who am I going to leave my fortune?"

"You've got a fortune?"

"Not yet, but I'm still young. Anything could happen."

They both laughed.

Chapter Ten

WHEN JOANNE CHECKED HER box at the Community Center postal hub, she'd received a package from Carla's mother…technically, Joanne's grandmother, although she certainly didn't feel familial toward the woman. She opened the package there on the long countertop provided for the residents' convenience. That way, if she didn't want it, she could simply discard it then and there.

The package contained a diary and a note:

Dear Joanne: I'm sorry for the way we left things, but it's simply too painful for me and Carl to be reminded not only of the daughter we no longer have with us but the fact that we never got to know our grandchild. Of course, we realize we could get to know you now, but we can't bear it yet. Hopefully, time will ease our pain, and we'll be able to meet with you. In the meantime, here is Carla's last diary so that maybe you can get to know your mother a bit better. — Best wishes, Louise

Joanne decided that if Carla was anything like her insensitive parents, she wasn't sure she wanted to get to know her better. She sighed, as she reflected on how, as a little girl, people would tell her she looked like Marion, her adoptive mom. Joanne had always known she'd been "specially chosen" by her parents, but she'd been flattered at the thought of resembling her dainty, beautiful mother.

And her dad had always made her laugh. There was never any crisis in which Dad couldn't elicit a smile amid her tears. Did she really want to read about Carla's life? Did it matter? She'd had the best parents anyone could've ever asked for.

She dropped the diary into her tote, took her car keys from her pocket, and went to see her Dad.

* * *

Greta went by the yoga studio where Kelsey and about ten other pretty, slender girls were sitting with their legs folded up like pretzels. She caught Kelsey's eye and gave her a wave. Kelsey straightened and came over to talk with Greta.

"Hi. Wanna join in?"

"Lord, have mercy, no, darlin'," Greta said. "If I did my legs like that, you'd have to carry me home in a wheelbarrow. I came to see if you'd like to learn how to make divinity."

"Divinity? What is that?"

"It's candy…kinda like meringue."

Kelsey's dark brows knit together. "Have you taught Justin how to make it?"

"Nope. And I won't be teaching you either. There's a new hot-shot candy maker getting ready to open up a shop here, and he'll be our teacher." Greta jerked her head. "Would you like to go meet him?"

"Sure. This class will be done in five minutes."

"All right. I'll wait for you in the hall."

When Kelsey emerged from the studio ten minutes later, she looked like she'd just stepped out of an ad for a fitness magazine. She wore a yellow tank top, black stretchy britches, and gray sneakers. Her damp hair had been pulled back into a ponytail, and she wore lip gloss and mascara. That's it. And yet, she glowed with youth and vitality. Greta would've been a little envious if she didn't love the girl. But she did, and she even managed to avoid telling Kelsey to enjoy her effortless looks while she could.

Greta led the way to Carson's Confectionery where the workers were still beating and banging like the dickens.

"Hello again!" Cade called to Greta.

"Hi, there! Is there any way we can talk for a minute out on one of the benches?"

"Sure." Cade came out of the shop and extended a hand to Kelsey. "Hi, I'm Cade."

"I'm Kelsey. Nice to meet you."

"This is your friend, Kelsey?" Cade asked Greta.

"Yes, sir, it is. Why do you sound so surprised? Did you think all my friends were of a certain age?"

Cade raised his hands in surrender. "No, ma'am."

"You'd better not," Kelsey said. "Greta is practically the queen of this place. Everybody loves her."

Greta grinned. "I pay her to say things like that. Let's talk for a second over there by the escalators. It's less noisy."

It was also where Justin should be coming by any minute now if he wasn't working overtime today.

They moved over to a bench by the escalators. Cade and Kelsey sat on one bench, and

Greta sat on the one adjacent to it.

"We're really hoping you can give us a lesson in divinity-making sometime soon," Greta said.

"All right. How about this evening?" Cade asked.

"Really? You'd work us in that quickly?" Greta was sure Kelsey's looks were helping their case.

"I really would." Cade smiled.

"Hi."

Yep. Justin was right on time, and he was almost to the bench where Kelsey sat when he spoke.

"Well, hi, darlin'," Greta said, as if it were such a pleasant surprise to see him there.

"How're you doing, Greta?" he asked.

"I'm as fine as I can be. Justin, this is Cade Carson. Cade's getting ready to open a new shop here at the Community Center."

Justin shook Cade's hand. "Justin Holmes. Nice to meet you."

"Nice to meet you too," Cade said.

"Kelsey, have you got plans later?" Justin asked.

"Um...yeah...I do. Maybe we can get together tomorrow or something?"

Justin rubbed his chin. "Yeah, sure." He paused, then said, "I'll see you guys later then."

* * *

Joanne found her dad sitting in the lobby of the residential care facility. There were a few other patients sitting around, and the television was on, but no one paid attention to it.

She went over to the sofa where her dad sat. "Hello."

He looked up at her and smiled. "Hello."

Joanne searched in vain for any spark of recognition. "I brought you a box of candy. May I sit with you?"

He scooted over and patted the cushion beside him. "I've got it warm for you."

She smiled as she sat. He used to say that often. Joanne handed him the box of assorted chocolates he'd always adored, and she watched his eyes light up. This withered member of Peter Pan's tribe of Lost Boys bore little resemblance to the robust man she'd grown up with.

Joanne sat beside him and took his hand. "Have you had your dinner yet?"

He nodded.

She still couldn't be sure if he'd eaten. She could go ask an attendant, but it didn't really matter. This candy made him happy, and surely, he could have some…especially, if she made sure he portioned it out. "Why don't you have three pieces now, and save the rest for later?"

He was too busy opening the box to answer.

"I need to talk to you," Joanne said. She knew he wouldn't really be paying attention to her, but she'd always gone to her daddy with her problems. She wanted to at least pretend that everything was normal, even if it only lasted a few precious minutes.

Joanne told her dad about Robert and Greta and Carla. She told him about Carla's parents and the diary. While she was talking, her dad slipped his bony hand into her tote and withdrew the diary.

"Read to me," he said.

"I don't think you want me to read *that* to you. I'll find something else."

"This! Read this to me." He opened the book and handed it to her. Then he sat back as expectantly as a four-year-old anticipating a fairy tale.

Joanne sighed, took the book, and read, "Today Robert Parker kissed me behind the bleachers after gym class."

Her dad laughed and popped a piece of chocolate into his mouth.

"Oh, you think that's funny?" Joanne said, with a grin.

He nodded. "Read more."

She looked back at the page. "It was my first kiss. I've liked Robert for such a long time, but I didn't know he felt the same way until today."

"Somebody has a crush," said Dad.

"Somebody does," she said.

"Did you write that?" he asked.

"No. My mother did."

"It's about her and your daddy?"

Tears pricked Joanne's eyes. "Maybe."

He nodded toward the box. "Can I have just one more piece?"

"Of course." She kissed his papery cheek.

Chapter Eleven

✿

GRETA USHERED KELSEY AND Cade into her kitchen. She'd assured Cade she had everything he'd need to make the candy. She loved to cook and kept her tiny pantry well stocked.

"Do you intend to offer candy-making classes in your shop?" she asked Cade.

"No, ma'am." He laughed. "That would kinda defeat my purpose, wouldn't it? I want people to buy my candy, not make their own."

"Then how did Greta talk you into teaching us how to make divinity?" Kelsey asked.

He blinked at her. "Have you met Greta?"

"Point taken." Kelsey laughed.

Greta wasn't about to let her idea get shot down so quickly. "Still, around the holidays, you could probably make some good extra income offering candy-making classes to families. Just use a couple of simple recipes that parents can make with their children." She nodded. "You could do something for Halloween and something for Christmas…and you could hold a couples' class for Valentine's Day."

"That would be so much fun!" Kelsey clasped her hands. "I think you should do it, Cade. It could help the residents get to know you."

"And, of course, you could go on the local television news programs and talk about the classes," Greta added. "That would be excellent publicity."

"Greta is great at marketing," Kelsey told Cade. "My yoga classes doubled in size on her word-of-mouth alone."

"I might have to hire you as my public relations manager," Cade said to Greta.

"I'll work for candy."

"You're hired."

Greta laughed and opened the cabinet doors. "Everything you need ingredient-wise should be in there, and if I can squeeze by you, I'll get you a saucepan."

When she handed him the saucepan, she asked if he lived at the Community Center.

"No, ma'am. I have a small house across town. Although, now that I see your apartment, I'm realizing that *small* is a relative term…no offense."

"None taken. Are you married?"

"No. I inherited the house from my uncle," Cade said. "Do I have to be married to have a house?"

"Certainly not. I'm just gathering information."

Kelsey shook her head. "You'll have to excuse us, Cade. We tend to be a little on the nosy side."

"How else can you get to know a person if you don't ask questions?" Greta asked.

"I agree." Cade took down the sugar canister. "Are either of you married?"

"Not me." Kelsey got out her phone and snapped a photo of the ingredients Cade had set out on the counter.

"No, but don't go falling for me, darlin'." Greta placed a hand on Cade's arm. "I'd probably end up breaking your heart."

He measured two cups of sugar into the saucepan. "Greta, I sized you up as a heartbreaker the minute I laid eyes on you."

Greta noticed that although Kelsey was using her phone to take recipe notes, she surreptitiously looked to see if she had any messages...presumably from Justin. She wondered what Justin was thinking right about now.

* * *

Back at home, Joanne made herself a ham-and-cheese sandwich and continued reading Carla's diary. Her dad had still been able to help her, and she thought that somewhere, somehow inside that muddled brain of his, he still knew she was his little girl. And he still knew how to make her feel better.

As she read, she began to feel as if she did know Carla—and, through her, Robert. They were no longer just cardboard cut-outs representing Joanne's biological parents. Joanne gained insight into Carla's parents too. Their daughter had been the center of their world. When Carla suffered her first mini stroke, she wrote about her parents' pain and their strength and how she hoped they didn't have to go through losing her.

Joanne read about Carla's affair with Winston Wallace. Carla had been so heartbroken over Robert's death, and Mr. Wallace had—in Carla's words—been devastated over his wife's miscarriage. But Joanne could see from what little her mother had written that Carla had been what today would be termed *groomed* by Mr. Wallace. The man might've been a brilliant attorney, but he had been a sexual predator to Carla...and likely to other girls as well.

Carla had stopped writing in the diary after she became pregnant. She'd written that she was terrified because she didn't think she'd be a good mother, and those pages bore tearstains and smudged ink. Joanne didn't know what had happened between her mother discovering she was pregnant and making the decision to give her away, because the next entry wasn't written until five years later and began, "I had another stroke."

Joanne was still absorbed in the pages of the diary when there was a knock at the door. She half-hoped it was Greta. She'd like to share the diary with Robert's mother, but she also wanted to read it through for herself first.

When she opened the door, she saw that it was Andrew. Her smile of surprise faded when she realized he was angry.

"Are you Winston Wallace's daughter?"

"I don't know...I might be."

"Why didn't you tell me why you really wanted to go to lunch with Margaret?" he demanded.

"Could you please come in, so my neighbors aren't privy to my business?" Joanne stepped aside so Andrew could come inside. She closed the door. "I did tell you why I wanted to have lunch with Margaret—to see if she remembered my mother."

"And to find out whether or not Mr. Wallace was your father."

"Margaret is the one who brought that up, not me."

Andrew ran his hands through his hair. "I like you, Joanne. A *lot*. I thought we could possibly have something special, but then I find out you might be suing Winston Wallace's estate. You could be putting the future of my firm in jeopardy."

"Who says I'm suing anyone? Because that thought never crossed my mind." Joanne clenched her fists. "I didn't begin the search for my biological parents in order to reap some sort of financial gain—as you, Margaret, and Eve Wallace seem to think. I wanted kinship...family."

Andrew's expelled a breath and then held out his arms. "Come here."

Joanne pointed at the door. "Get out."

"But—"

"Now!"

As soon as she could be sure he was gone, Joanne grabbed her keys and her phone and hurried to Greta's apartment.

* * *

Greta popped a piece of her half of the divinity into her mouth and thought, *Sorry, Cade. Mine's better.* She wondered if she should give him a couple of pointers but decided to wait for a bit. She didn't want to insult the man. After all, he'd just spent the evening giving her and Kelsey a free divinity-making lesson.

She turned the TV to the channel guide to see what was coming on. When her phone rang, she answered it and heard only sobbing.

She froze. *Oh, no…Kelsey. My plan to make Justin jealous must've blown up in Kelsey's poor little face.* "Honey, calm down. Whatever it is, we can fix it."

"I'm…not…so…sure."

That's not Kelsey. "Joanne?"

"Yes."

"Where are you?"

"Almost at your door."

Greta hopped off the couch and hurried to the door. She flung it open to see Joanne headed her way. She closed the distance between them and enveloped the girl in a hug. "Everything's gonna be all right. I promise. What happened?"

"I…threw…Andrew…out."

Greta led Joanne into the apartment and over to the sofa. "Here…sit down and relax. What did he do? Did he get fresh with you?"

Joanne shook her head. "N-no. He th-thinks the same thing Eve Wallace does…that I'm a m-money g-grubber."

"Then I'm glad you threw him out." She sat beside Joanne and hugged her while she wept.

Chapter Twelve

ON WEDNESDAY MORNING, JOANNE was soaking in her bathtub. She had lavender-scented Epsom salts in the water, a rolled towel behind her neck, and a de-puffing mask on her eyes. She thought about how nice it had been to be in Greta's apartment last night. Once Joanne had calmed down, they'd snacked on divinity, biscotti, and decaffeinated coffee.

They'd talked about Robert, and Joanne had told Greta about the diary.

"I'll bring it to you to read," Joanne had said.

Greta shook her head. "No, thank you, darlin'. That's yours. It's private—between you and your mother."

Sometime later, Andrew had called, and Joanne had declined to answer.

"Was that him?" Greta had asked.

Joanne nodded.

"Do you like him?"

"I did before he accused me of being a gold-digger. But maybe it's best that it ended before it ever really got started."

"I don't know…you might want to consider letting him grovel a little and then giving him another chance."

Joanne smiled now at the memory. She hadn't been ready to listen to anything Andrew had to say last night—whether he'd wanted to apologize or give his reasons for flinging his crass accusations—but she'd consider talking with him today…if he called.

When her phone rang a few minutes later, it was eerie. It was like she'd reached him telepathically or something. She got out of the tub, flung the eye mask onto the sink, wrapped a towel around her, and picked up the phone. All of this only to discover that it wasn't Andrew after all. It was the pharmacy.

She stifled a groan, hoping they didn't need her to come in. "Hello?"

"Joanne, hi, it's Leslie. This guy named Andrew just called here for you and said it's urgent."

Frowning, she wondered what could be so important. "All right, thanks. I'll call him back."

As soon as she ended the call from Leslie, she called Andrew.

He answered with, "Joanne…thank God."

"What's wrong? And why didn't you call my cell?"

"When you never answered me last night, I figured you'd blocked my number. Is there any way you can get over here?"

"Over where?" she asked.

"To my office. Your grandmother is over here going berserk."

* * *

"Your crocodile tears don't bother me in the least, missy," Greta told Margaret. "For Pete's sake, you've worked in a law firm for the better part of your life, and you don't have the good sense to keep your mouth shut and not spread idle gossip?"

Standing in front of Margaret's desk with her hands on her hips, Greta gave the woman approximately three seconds to respond. When she didn't, Greta lit into her again.

"You'll be lucky if my granddaughter doesn't sue you for the defamation of her mother's character."

"But Carla and Mr. Wallace—"

Greta put up her hand. "I don't want to hear it. The law firm I employ is bigger and better than this one ever dared to be, and I won't rest until—"

Someone gently placed a hand on her arm, and Greta whirled to give this new person what-for. She'd done sent Andrew packing. Who had they sent down here now?

"Oh! Joanne!" She gave Joanne a brief hug. "What're you doing here, darlin'?" She waved her hands. "Never mind that now." She turned back to Margaret, who was backing her chair away from her desk. "Where do you think *you're* going? Joanne's here now, so you can start apologizing."

"Ma'am, I think you'd better come with us."

This time when Greta turned, she saw two uniformed police officers approaching.

She glared at Margaret. "You people are a bunch of cowards. You run your mouth about things you know nothing about and then call the police when you have to answer for what you've done."

"Greta, please," Joanne said, softly.

One of the police officers, a young man who barely looked old enough to shave, took hold of Greta's upper arm. "Come on."

"Don't you get rough with me, mister," Greta said. "How would it look on your record that you manhandled a helpless old lady who's probably not in her right mind?" She thought it couldn't hurt to get started on an insanity plea, just in case.

"I might agree with that last part," the officer said, "but you're a far cry from helpless."

Greta linked her arm through his. "Sassy. I like that in a man."

He grinned and shook his head as he escorted her from the building.

* * *

"What will they do to her?" Joanne asked.

"I don't know, and I don't care," Margaret said. "In fact, I hope they throw the book at her."

Joanne narrowed her eyes. "I still haven't heard that apology yet. And for someone who seemed so proud of her discretion, you sure couldn't wait to tell Mrs. Wallace and Andrew your suspicions. And my grandmother really *does* have a huge law firm on retainer."

She didn't know whether that was true or not, but she hoped it was. Greta might need a good attorney to get her out of this mess.

"Fine." Margaret stood, and sent her chair rolling backward. "I'm sorry." She opened her mouth to say more, but Andrew interrupted them.

"Sorry I couldn't get back down here sooner," he said. "I had a client on the phone. Are you okay?"

Even though he was addressing Joanne, Margaret answered.

"Yes, I'm fine. That woman—"

"What will they do to her?" Joanne asked Andrew.

He draped his arm around her and walked her outside where Greta was talking—and laughing—with the officers.

"Is she going to have to do hard time?" Andrew asked them.

"No. Ms. Parker doesn't have a record and has promised to vacate the premises and not return...and we believe she'll keep her word," the young officer said.

Nodding at the arm Andrew still had around Joanne's shoulders, the other officer said, "If she's as feisty as her grandmother, good luck to you."

"I need all the luck I can get right now, sir," Andrew said.

"Greta, are you ready to go back home?" Joanne asked.

"I guess I'd better. I have a date tonight, and I don't want Steve having to come visit me at the jailhouse."

"We'll see you to your car, Ms. Parker," the younger officer said.

"See you back at the Center!" Greta called to Joanne.

"I know you need to go," Andrew said. "But would you please check at the pharmacy before you go to your apartment? I didn't realize you had the day off."

"Okay." She kissed his cheek. "Thanks for calling me. I know it took me a few minutes to get here, but I came as quickly as I could."

"I didn't know what else to do. Your grandma is a wild woman."

Joanne smiled. *Her grandmother.* "Yeah. She is."

Chapter Thirteen

GRETA'S ADRENALINE RUSH HAD ended by the time she arrived at the Kinsey Falls Living and Retail Community Center. Had she overreacted? Embarrassed Joanne in front of the young man she was dating? Joanne had seemed all right when Greta had left the law firm, but maybe she wasn't. Maybe she wouldn't even want to speak to Greta again.

She sank onto a bench outside of Nothin' But Knit. She had a clear view of the doors here, and she could catch Joanne and apologize as soon as she arrived at the Community Center.

"Hey."

Greta looked up to see that the soft voice belonged to Jade. Had she not been so focused on the entrance, she'd have realized that. "Hi, doll. How are you?"

"I'm fine. I came to see if you are." She sat beside Greta on the bench. "I'm not used to seeing you sitting in one place unless you have knitting needles in your hands. Is everything okay?"

"I don't know." Greta gave Jade an abridged version of what had taken place at the law firm.

"That's a pretty wild story." Jade's lips twisted, as she tried not to smile.

"I'm afraid Joanne is upset with me…but I'm hoping that if I try to talk with her out here, she at least won't yell at me in front of everybody. Maybe she'll give me a chance to explain."

Jade gave Greta a one-armed hug. "I think what you did was admirable."

"It must be my lucky day," said Caleb Young, Jade's beau, who worked at the pet shop across from Nothin' But Knit. "I look up from my post at Hightail It! and see two beautiful women just a paper-airplane flight from my door. So, I got Aidan to watch the register while I came out to make sure everybody is okay."

"Now look what you've done," Jade told Greta. "You went and got Caleb in save-the-damsel-in-distress mode."

"Well, now, I'm perfectly all right, but if Caleb wants to sweep me up in those big, strong arms of his and carry me off, I might be able to work up a swoon." Greta waggled her eyebrows to drive home her point.

Caleb laughed. "I can see you're fine, Greta." He gave Jade a quick peck on the lips before heading back to the pet shop.

"That's a good man you have there," Greta said.

"Yes, he is." Jade dragged her eyes back to Greta. "How about you? You've got a good man, too, from what I hear."

"Yes. Steve is a peach. He's taking me to bingo Friday night."

"Caleb and I will see you there then," Jade said. "I'm glad they made bingo night a monthly thing after the grand opening celebration. I've come to really enjoy them, and Caleb has been hooked ever since he won free muffins for a week from the café."

"Is Terri coming?"

"I think so." Jade frowned slightly. "I doubt Mitch will come with her, though. He likes to pretend that everyone will recognize him and fawn all over him if he shows up. I've yet to see that happen anywhere else. I don't know why bingo night should be any different."

"You don't seem to think Mitch and Terri are a good match."

Jade looked over her shoulder to see that her partner was engaged with a customer. "I just hope she isn't getting too serious about him."

Before Jade could elaborate, Joanne came in.

She strode over to the bench and looked down at Greta with tears in her eyes.

Greta hopped up off the bench. "Oh, Joanne, I'm sorry."

Joanne hugged her. "For what? You took up for me. Thank you."

"I'd better get back, guys," Jade said. "See you later." She gave them a little wave and hurried back to Nothin' But Knit.

"You aren't upset with me?" Greta asked.

"No." Joanne smiled slightly. "I mean, you might've gone a little overboard, but you went there as my grandmother. That...that's awesome."

"Why don't we go upstairs and have some tea? Or do you need to go to work?"

"I need to go by the pharmacy, but I don't have to work today," Joanne said. "I'll be up there soon."

* * *

Joanne couldn't keep from smiling as she walked to the pharmacy. Greta had not only accepted her as a part of her family, but she'd defended Joanne like a momma bear with a threatened cub. Not only that, Andrew had sent her flowers. She hoped they'd arrived—she could hardly wait to see them.

She navigated the aisles of shampoo and cosmetics to get to the back of the store where the pharmacy was located. Leslie, the other pharmacy tech, grinned at Joanne.

"Somebody's got a boyfriend," Leslie said, in a singsong voice.

Joanne blushed but was pleased. Leslie, with her dark hair and big brown eyes, was always talking about her dates. Joanne was glad to have a little attention thrown her way.

Leslie nodded toward the counter at a beautiful bouquet of pink and white roses in a clear vase.

"For me?" Joanne asked, making sure that these were, in fact, the flowers sent from Andrew.

"All yours."

"Aren't they gorgeous?" Joanne gingerly picked up the vase.

"Yes, they are. If you kick him to the curb, let me know, will ya?" Leslie winked and got back to work.

Joanne was a little self-conscious as she walked through the store to the postal center, carrying the flowers. Several people turned to look, and a couple of women commented on how pretty they were.

She placed the vase on the counter while she opened her mailbox. As she rifled through her mail, she called Andrew.

"Hi, there," he answered. "I take it they've arrived?"

"They have, and they're beautiful. Thank you so much."

"You're welcome."

"I'm really sorry Greta made such a scene at your office this morning."

Andrew laughed. "Nonsense. She's given us all something to talk about for the rest of the day. Besides, what she said was right—Margaret had no business saying what she did. She acted as if she'd known for sure that you were Winston Wallace's daughter and that you were out for financial gain. That was uncalled for." He cleared his throat. "My behavior last night was uncalled for as well. I jumped to the same conclusion and acted like a jerk."

"That's fine."

"I'm forgiven?"

"Completely."

"Good. When can I see you again?" he asked.

"Well, Friday is bingo night here at the Community Center."

"You want me to play bingo with a bunch of golden oldies?"

"It's not just the golden oldies. Everyone who likes to win stuff goes," Joanne said. "Of course, if you don't like winning stuff, then I can see you—"

"I'll be there."

She laughed as she ended the call and tossed her junk mail in the recycling bin. She flipped through the envelopes that remained: bill, bill...the test results.

The very sight of the envelope turned her blood cold. She dropped the phone and her unopened mail into her purse and retrieved her flowers. She'd open the envelope upstairs in her apartment. She'd paid extra to get the results expedited, but she hadn't expected them this soon.

This time, as she walked through the Community Center, she paid no attention to anyone. She was too focused on getting home to receive the news that would—in one way or another—be life changing.

Once inside her apartment, Joanne quickly put the vase of flowers on the kitchen table and dropped her purse into a chair. She took out the unopened envelope with the results of the paternity test. She wondered momentarily if she should take the envelope to Greta's, so they could read the results together. But, no. She needed to do this alone. She dropped the envelope onto the table and took a deep, steadying breath.

* * *

Greta had stopped in at the café to get a cappuccino before heading up to her apartment. She felt like celebrating, and a vanilla cappuccino with extra whipped cream would sure hit the spot.

As soon as Greta stepped out of the café, Kelsey hugged her and came in a hair knocking that cappuccino right out of Greta's hand.

"Sorry!" Kelsey said, breathlessly. "It didn't spill, did it?"

"No, darlin', it's fine. What's the matter?"

"Nothing—I just ran all the way over here from the yoga studio when I saw you going into the café. I didn't want to miss you."

Greta squinted. "The way you're grinning reminds me of the cat that swallowed the cream."

Kelsey giggled. "Justin called me this morning and asked to take me to breakfast. We ate here in the café, and he told me he really likes me and that he wants to take me on a real date. He's tired of us hanging in the friend zone."

This time Greta initiated the hug. "Well, hallelujah! It's about time."

"I know, right? But I'm not getting my hopes up yet," Kelsey said.

"Yes, you are, and that's fine. Hopes belong way up in the air."

The young woman inclined her head. "Your timing yesterday when we were talking with Cade...did that have anything to do with when Justin usually gets home from work?"

"Oh, now, come on. Do you really think I'm that crafty?" Greta asked.

"I do. And I love you for it."

Greta was humming a mindless tune as she walked to her apartment. Joanne called to say that something had come up and that she'd be delayed a little while.

"Take your time, sweetie," Greta said. But there was something in Joanne's tone that worried her.

Chapter Fourteen

❂

J OANNE REREAD THE PATERNITY test results as tears dripped onto the single sheet of paper. She and Greta weren't related. Greta would be heartbroken. As far as she was concerned, she hadn't needed the results to feel as if she were Joanne's grandmother. She'd gone right down to the law firm and had given anyone who'd listen a piece of her mind.

She smiled and wiped her eyes. Joanne had desperately wanted Robert to be her father. She sighed and looked down at the paper again. One couldn't argue with science. Robert Parker was not her biological father, and Greta wasn't her grandmother.

More than likely, Winston Wallace was her biological father. Should she have Eve obtain a DNA sample from her daughter to confirm? What would that even accomplish? The Wallaces' daughter probably wouldn't want a sisterly relationship with the child he'd had while cheating on her mother with another woman.

Still…it was better to know the truth about her biological parents. Wasn't it? Learning the identity of her biological parents was what had led her on this quest to begin with. She couldn't simply abandon her search this close to knowing. Could she?

She picked up her phone and called Eve Wallace.

* * *

When Greta opened the door to find Millie—rather than Joanne—standing there, her face fell.

"Well, don't look so delighted to see me," Millie said. "I might never leave."

"I'm sorry. I was expecting Joanne." She stepped back. "Please come on in. Would you like some coffee or tea?"

"No, thanks. Jade called and told me about your visit to the law firm. I had to come hear the tale firsthand." She sat on the sofa and smiled at Greta.

Greta sank onto the cushion beside her. "Oooh, Millie, knowing that woman—Margaret—was spreading lies about Carla and Joanne flew all over me. The more I thought about it last night, the madder I got. So, this morning, I went down there."

Millie slipped her shoes off and put her feet up on the ottoman. "I just want to settle in. Please continue."

"That woman told everybody Joanne's private business and made all those highfalutin people think that Joanne was some money-grubbing daughter of a hussy." Greta pressed her lips together and shook her head. "You know good and well Joanne isn't like that. She wants one thing—family. At least, I have you, Steve, and the friends I've made since moving here. I don't think Joanne has anyone."

"I know you told me her mother was dead and that her father had dementia," Millie said. "But, surely, she has some friends."

"I don't believe she has anyone she's really close to. It appears to me that she took care of her parents until her mother died and her father's condition deteriorated to the point that she had to move him into a professional care facility. So, here she comes to Kinsey Falls looking for family and gets almost every door she knocks on slammed in her face."

"Not yours." Millie smiled softly.

"No, not mine. But I think I must've embarrassed her or gotten her into trouble or something with my visit to the law firm."

"Why's that?"

"Joanne was supposed to come over, but she called and told me something had come up and that she'd be later than she'd expected to be."

"So? That doesn't mean she isn't coming. It means she's going to be late and didn't want you worrying about it."

"We'll see," Greta said.

"I'm surprised at you. Since we moved here, you've become the very personification of optimism. Now, with something as important as your relationship with your granddaughter, you're turning into a pessimist?"

"What if it turns out she's not Robert's daughter?"

"At this point, does it even matter?" Millie asked.

"Not to me, it doesn't."

Millie squeezed Greta's hand. "Then make sure Joanne knows that."

* * *

Eve's apartment was every bit as perfect as Joanne had imagined it would be. She'd replaced the living room furniture that came standard with every other Community Center apartment with a white sofa, a large pink-and-white damask ottoman, and a dusty-rose wingback chair. A pair of two-tiered maple end tables had been placed at either side of the sofa. The current issue of a fashion magazine lay on the bottom shelf of the table closest to the fireplace.

"Won't you sit down?" Eve asked.

She wore turquoise palazzo pants and a white silk tunic, and her hair and makeup were flawless. Joanne thought she must be going out somewhere.

"I won't keep you but a moment," Joanne said.

Eve gave an elegant shrug. "Nonsense. I've made us some peach tea." She walked into the kitchen and brought back a bone china tea set on a wicker serving tray. She placed the tray on the ottoman, poured a cup of tea, and handed it to Joanne. "Help yourself to sugar and milk."

Joanne took a single sugar cube and watched it begin to melt into the tea. She noticed that Eve took her tea plain.

"You said over the phone that you received the results of the Parker paternity test," Eve said. "I'm guessing it was negative, or you wouldn't be here."

"That's right. Robert Parker was not my biological father."

"Which means that, more than likely, my husband was." She lifted her chin. "Now what?"

"I'm sorry, Ms. Wallace. I wish with all my heart that Robert *had* been my father."

"Right...but you still want my daughter's DNA to prove that..." Eve took a deep breath. "That you're her...her sister."

"Half-sister." Joanne hung her head. *Was* that what she wanted? Two scenarios played out back-to-back in her mind. In the first, a young woman close to Joanne's age and appearance flings open the front door of a house and embraces Joanne enthusiastically. The woman's husband—in Joanne's mind, a bearded version of Andrew, for some reason—brings over their baby girl and hands her to Joanne. It's a scene of sisterly bliss.

In the second scenario—the one Joanne felt would be the most likely—that same young woman takes one look at Joanne, barrels out the door, and pushes her. She yells terrible things about both Joanne and Carla. This young woman is filled with anger and resentment, and Joanne knows she'll never be accepted as a member of her family.

"What are you thinking?" Eve asked softly.

Her quiet, cultured voice brought Joanne out of her reverie. "Your daughter would despise me, wouldn't she?"

"Amber is mature enough to realize that you had no control over what your mother and my...and Winston did. She'd be disillusioned with Winston...and she'd despise your mother. Feeling that your mother seduced Winston would be the only way she could forgive him for what he did. She'd have to paint him as the victim of some temptress…whether it was the truth or not."

Joanne refrained from saying that Carla had certainly not been a temptress and that her diary could prove it. What good would that do at this point?

"Carla wasn't the first," Eve continued. "Nor was she the last. But I wouldn't want Amber to know that. I can't even recall meeting your mother." She shook her head slightly. "Imagine how you'd feel if someone told you she was the daughter of your father and a woman with whom he'd had an affair. How would you feel about her?"

Remembering the sweet relationship her father and mother had shared, Joanne doubted that could ever happen. But, then, she didn't know anything about Eve's relationship with Winston. Maybe he was good to her—loved her, even—but thought extra-marital trysts were all right. Who knows? Who can ever tell what's going on in someone else's mind?

But if someone *had* ever come to her and said she was her dad's love child, she couldn't fathom welcoming that person into her life.

"We could never be like sisters…or even friends," Joanne said.

"No. I'm afraid not." Eve sipped her tea. "I can probably come up with some sort of ruse to get a sample of her DNA. As I told you, I'll be seeing her this weekend."

Joanne shook her head. "That won't be necessary. I'd just like you to do me one favor."

Eve stiffened. "What's that?"

"When your daughter comes to visit, I'd like to meet her. Introduce me to her as a friend you've made here at the Community Center. If you can come up with a ruse to get a DNA sample, then that one should be no problem."

"Why?"

"I'd just like to see her."

"You won't tell her who you are?" Eve asked.

"No." She smiled. "We don't know for sure anyway."

Eve let out a breath of relief. "Then it'll be my pleasure to introduce you."

* * *

Greta looked down at her phone when it rang. "It's Joanne."

"Take it," Millie said. "I'll talk with you tomorrow."

"No, wait." Greta answered the call, as Millie perched on the edge of the chair, unsure whether she should leave or not. "Hey, darlin'."

"Greta, hi," Joanne said. "I'm sorry, but I'm not going to be able to come over tonight. I have a headache and I'm going to lie down."

"Oh. All right. I hope you feel better."

"Thanks."

"If you need me—no matter what time it is—call me," Greta said. "And I'll be right there to help however I can."

There was a pause…Greta would have called it a *weighty* pause because she wondered if Joanne really had a headache or merely didn't want to see her.

"I appreciate that," Joanne said at last.

Greta ended the call and turned back to Millie, her eyes swimming with tears. "She doesn't want to talk with me. I really messed up today, and she—"

"Don't jump to conclusions." Millie leaned forward and squeezed Greta's hand. "What did she say?"

"That she had a headache and was going to lie down."

"Then maybe she has a headache and is going to lie down."

Greta shook her head. "I don't think so. Or, even if she does, I think it's more than that. Maybe she thinks I'm some old kook that she wants nothing to do with, even if I *am* her grandmother…and I might not even be that."

"Gee…that's impressive."

"What is?"

"You don't only jump to conclusions," Millie said, "but you're able to leap over the mountains you've made out of molehills."

"Fine, Ms. CCC." Greta sometimes referred to her friend as Ms. Calm, Cool, and Collected—Ms. CCC. "Tell me what you think I should do."

"Don't worry about it tonight. Take the girl at her word. Then tomorrow go and talk with her. Tell her your concerns."

"What if she says, 'Yep, Greta, you're a kook, and I want you to stay the heck away from me?'"

"Then stay the heck away from her and realize you're better off without her. There are a lot of people who love you. Me, included."

"But I want *her* to love me too. I want to be her grandmother."

Millie's voice softened. "I know. I want that too."

"Okay, so now that we have a plan in place, let's not be maudlin. I have some good news. Kelsey said Justin asked her out on a proper date." She smiled. "They're together."

"That's fantastic. Your plan worked. But now what are you going to do about poor Cade? He might've really liked Kelsey."

"Nah, they weren't right for each other. I've got him in mind for Terri...that is, if he doesn't have a girlfriend."

"Terri? You're throwing him at her? When I'm sitting here single and ready to mingle?"

Greta scoffed. "Since when?"

"Since a gorgeous man who can make candy moved into the building."

"Who do you think you are—*me?*"

"I've decided if you can be a flirt, so can I." Millie threw back her head and laughed.

"You know, if you're serious about being ready to mingle, I can talk with Steve and—"

"No, thank you. If I can't have Cade, I don't want anyone...unless that granddad who taught him how to make candy is still around. He might be interesting."

Greta knew Millie was kidding, but she couldn't help but wonder if Cade's grandfather *were* still around...and if he was single.

* * *

When Joanne's doorbell rang, she hurried to the kitchen and got an ice pack from the freezer. Her head wasn't hurting, but if Greta was here, she wanted to put on a good show. Drawing her brows together in what she hoped was an expression of pain, she opened the door.

It was Andrew.

"Jo, are you all right?"

Jo. Where did that *come from?*

She brightened. "I'm better now. Come on in and have a seat while I put this ice pack back into the freezer. May I get you something to drink?"

"No, thanks, I'm fine. I just came to check on you." Rather than sitting down, he followed her into the kitchen.

"Greta didn't call you, did she?" she asked, as she returned the ice pack to the freezer.

"No." He chuckled. "Is she going to?"

"I was afraid she'd called to tell you I had a headache and was lying down."

His mouth turned down at the corners. "That sounds like something she would say is my fault. Are you feeling better?"

Joanne smiled slightly. "Yes…and no. I never really had a headache. I just didn't want to talk with Greta tonight."

"Are you upset about what she did today?"

"No, that's not it at all. I actually think that was kinda cool…that she was that determined to protect a granddaughter she barely knows."

"I think it's cool, too. I'd sure rather be on Greta Parker's good side than her bad one. Any ideas on how I can sway her?"

Joanne shook her head as tears filled her eyes.

"Hey, hey, hey." Andrew pulled her into his arms and kissed the top of her head. "What's wrong?"

"Greta isn't my grandmother," she whispered.

He led her into the living room to the sofa. "Let's sit down and talk about it. Are you sure?"

She nodded.

"And what? She's through with you now?"

His voice had an edge to it, and Joanne didn't want him to be angry at Greta.

"No. She doesn't even know yet."

Andrew stroked her hair for a minute. Joanne knew he was trying to understand, but she was having trouble understanding her feelings herself. How could she explain them to someone else? That's why she hadn't gone to see Greta tonight.

"I know you're disappointed," he said. "And she will be too."

"Please don't say anything."

"I won't. I barely know Greta—"

"No…I mean at work." Joanne pulled back, so she could look Andrew in the eye. "The fact that I'm not Robert Parker's daughter means my father is probably Winston Wallace. I've spoken with Eve, and I'm not going to publicize that fact. It would only hurt her daughter."

He nodded. "My lips are sealed."

She pressed her head against his chest. "I came to Kinsey Falls looking for family. And I thought I'd found exactly what I was looking for."

"Sweetheart, you did."

"But will Greta feel that way when she learns I'm not her son's child?"

Chapter Fifteen

❀

WHEN GRETA WOKE THURSDAY morning, her first thought was of Joanne. How was she feeling? She hoped she hadn't had a migraine. But she hoped that Joanne hadn't been lying about the headache and was avoiding her.

Great! Now I feel bad because I want *my granddaughter to have had a headache!*

She quickly bathed, dressed, and put on a little makeup. Then she went to Joanne's apartment. If Joanne was feeling up to it, Greta was planning to buy her breakfast. When Joanne didn't answer the door, Greta thought she must be at work already. Normally, she'd call her at this point, but she wanted to talk with Joanne face to face.

Greta took the stairs to the lower level and walked to the pharmacy. She was delaying her morning walk, so she might as well get in a little cardio while she could.

The store manager had just opened the gate and was heading back to his office when Greta entered the front part of the pharmacy. They exchanged greetings before Greta headed toward the back.

She saw Joanne working there behind the counter. Joanne looked up and smiled. And then her eyes widened, and she covered her mouth with her hand.

* * *

Joanne had been pleased to see Greta walk in. She'd been planning to ask her to dinner later so they could talk about everything.

But now...this.

A young man in a black hoodie with a red bandana pulled up over his nose and mouth grabbed Greta from behind and pressed a knife to her throat. "I want your oxy...all of it you've got. Now!"

Joanne lowered her trembling hand from her mouth. "P-please...I'll give you...whatever you want. J-just let her g-go."

"I'm all right," Greta said.

"Shut up! Both of you!"

"S-she's m-my grandmother! Let her go!"

"Give me the oxy, and I won't cut her."

Joanne heard Leslie's voice behind her. "I'm getting it! See? I'm working on it right now."

Greta stared at Joanne before closing her eyes for a millisecond.

She's going to do something stupid. Greta, please don't! But if I say something—

Greta's fist came up behind her and her thumbnail dug into her assailant's cheek. At the same time, she pulled down the arm holding the knife while striking at him again with her left hand.

Joanne's scream mingled with the robber's curses. Greta fell to the floor, and the young man lashed out with a vicious kick. Greta didn't make a sound. Nor did she move.

"Greta!" Joanne cried.

"Give me the oxy, or this old lady won't be the only one hurt."

"This is all we have," Leslie said, putting a bag of OxyContin tablets on the counter.

The robber swiped the bag off the counter and turned to leave, but two police officers—guns drawn—were coming through the entrance. He looked for another way out, but when one of the officers threatened to shoot him, he dropped the knife and the drugs and surrendered.

The store manager was near the officers. "Is everyone all right?" He looked down at Greta, who rolled over, wincing in pain. "Thank goodness, I saw this whole thing about to go down on the security cam and that these officers were in the café when the call came in."

One of the officers was the young man who'd been at the law firm escorting Greta from the building. While his partner was handcuffing her assailant, he stooped down and grinned at Greta. "You'd do anything to see me again, wouldn't you?"

"What can I say, kid? When you've got it, you've got it. Now, help me up, would you?"

He shook his head. "You're gonna stay right where you're at until the paramedics get here. Don't move."

"I don't need a paramedic."

"Let's let them be the judge of that." He winked. "Besides, it makes them feel important."

"If you weren't such a pretty young 'un, I'd get up from here and smack you."

"Good thing I'm pretty." He laughed.

"Hey, pretty boy," his partner called. "Can you give me a hand here?"

Joanne fell to her knees beside Greta, tears dripping off her chin. "I'm so sorry. Are you all right?"

Greta tried once again to sit up, but Joanne put a hand on her shoulder to restrain her.

"No! They said you can't move. The paramedics are—"

"We're here," said a woman with an authoritative voice. "Could everyone move out of the way, please?"

"I could, if somebody would give me a hand," Greta said. "I'm a little dizzy. It's not every day I have to fight drug addicts." She shook her head. "Bless his heart. I wonder if he has a bad home life. I should make him some cookies."

"Grandma! That man had a knife to your throat!"

The woman took Greta's blood pressure, and then she and her

partner—a muscular man with a wolf tattoo on his forearm—put Greta on a backboard.

"Hi, honey," Greta said to the man. "I'm glad you're here. I don't think she could carry me by herself. I feel safer now." Then she looked at Joanne. "Hey! You called me *grandma!*"

Joanne smiled through her tears. "I did."

"Would you like to ride with your grandmother to the hospital?" the woman EMT asked.

"Yes, please."

"By all means," the store manager said. "And take the rest of the day off."

The paramedics picked Greta up.

"Have you got me, Wolfman?" she asked.

"I've got you, Little Red."

* * *

Greta's left leg ached where the robber had kicked her. And it was as embarrassing as heck to be carried out of the Community Center like some kind of invalid. Everyone stopped and stared. She hoped none of her friends were in the crowd. She'd hate for them to think she was a wuss who couldn't defend herself. Because the truth was that she *had* defended herself. The skills that Renshi Max had taught to the Silver Sleuths had served her well. She'd have to let him know...and maybe bake him a cake or something.

Once she was loaded into the ambulance, Joanne took her hand. "How are you?"

"My leg hurts. I'm lucky that kid was wearing sneakers instead of steel-toed boots."

"When I saw you lying there...not moving..."

"Oh, darlin', I'm sorry I scared you. I was lying low, so the kid didn't feel I was a threat," Greta said. "But if he'd tried to come across that counter to get you, I'd have got up from there and clobbered him." She thought maybe that sentence came from a place of bravado rather than truth. "Or, I'd have done my best."

She looked up at Wolfman, and he grinned. He was a looker. Wonder who she could fix him up with?

"I don't think anything is broken, but you probably have a bone bruise…and your left thigh is likely one huge contusion," said Wolfman. "No more crime fighting for you for a while."

"Did you make sure she wasn't cut?" Joanne asked him.

He nodded. "Not a scratch."

Greta smiled. "Renshi Max will be so proud."

"Renshi Max? He's my karate instructor."

"He's a good guy," Greta said.

Wolfman agreed.

Fatigue hit her like a tsunami. With her free hand, she patted Wolfman's forearm. Her eyelids were drooping.

"It's all right," Wolfman said. "What you're feeling right now is a letdown after the adrenaline rush. Just rest until we get you to the hospital."

She was aware of voices around her: Joanne, Wolfman, the other EMT. But she couldn't tell what they were saying. She wasn't sure she really cared at the moment…

* * *

Joanne sat by Greta's bed in the emergency room. There were people all around, checking Greta's vitals and asking a lot of questions to which Joanne had no answers.

Greta's eyelids fluttered.

"Hi, there," Joanne said softly.

"Hi. What did I miss?"

Before Joanne could answer, a perky nurse came into the room with a hospital gown. "Hi, Ms. Parker, if you could, put this on please. We'll get you down to radiology soon to see about that leg."

Greta rolled her eyes at Joanne.

"I'll be right outside," Joanne said. "Call if you need me."

When Greta was changed, the nurse said two orderlies would be in soon to wheel her down to radiology. Joanne returned to the chair by the bed.

"I hate this," Greta said. "I want to go home."

"I know…and we'll get you there as soon as possible."

"So…was your head really hurting last night?"

Joanne lowered her gaze. "No. I got the test results back."

"And you don't belong to Robert."

She looked up at Greta. "You don't seem surprised."

"If you'd had happy news, you wouldn't have sounded so glum about it. Oh, well, we knew all along that was a possibility, didn't we?"

"Yeah. I guess that's it then."

"You guess that's what?"

Joanne shrugged one shoulder. "I'm not your granddaughter."

"I beg to differ. You told that robber I was your grandmother. And you even called me *Grandma* once, unless my ears were playing tricks on me."

"I did call you *Grandma*."

"Well, all right then. Your mother and my son thought the world of each other, and had he lived, I have no doubt in my mind that they'd have gotten married. You would have been my granddaughter then by blood. But someone said once—and I'm old, so forgive me if I misquote—blood makes you related, but love makes you family."

There came a sharp tap on the door. "Orderlies! Here to take Ms. Parker to radiology."

"Give me a second please," she called. She smiled at Joanne. "I'm not done. You were chosen once by two people who wanted you and welcomed you into a wonderful family. I'd like to choose you to be my granddaughter."

Joanne couldn't speak for the lump in her throat. She merely nodded and hugged her grandmother.

* * *

Greta smiled to see Steve waiting with Joanne in the hallway when she stepped out of the emergency room. "I'm so glad to see you."

He was in front of her with one step and pulled her into a bear hug. Then he quickly loosened his grip. "I didn't hurt you, did I?"

"Nah, I'm tough as nails."

"If I had five minutes with that little punk—"

Greta shook her head. "Look forward, not back." She was already wondering how she might be able to help the young man. He obviously had a ton of problems...but she couldn't dwell on that right now. "Let's go home."

She later learned that Terri had called Steve as soon as she'd found out about what happened. Terri had been in the knitting room and had been one of the few people at Kinsey Falls Living and Retail Community Center who hadn't seen Greta being carted out on a backboard, but Jade had seen her. And Jade had told Millie. Millie had called Cade. Kelsey had run out of her yoga studio when all the excitement had happened, and she called Justin. Gilda had been outside walking Moonshine, so she'd called the Silver Sleuths.

And now, as Greta was walking into the Community Center, there they all were. Smiles, hugs, flowers, candy, balloons—Greta felt like one of those little Hadid girls.

Epilogue

THE BALLROOM WAS CROWDED as Greta and Steve looked around for Joanne and Terri. Andrew was tall, so he finally stood up and waved to them.

"Goodness," Greta said. "It's packed tonight." She hugged Terri and Joanne while Steve shook hands with Andrew. "Where's Mitch?"

"He couldn't make it."

"Well, then, we have room at our table for one more." Greta grinned, as she turned and beckoned to Cade.

Steve smiled. He wholeheartedly approved.

Greta made the introductions, and they all sat back down at their table. She rubbed her hands together as she looked down at her card. "I feel lucky tonight."

"You always say that, and you never win," Steve said.

"I don't need to win at bingo to be lucky." She scrunched up her nose at him,

He gave her a peck on the cheek. "Neither do I...but I wouldn't say no to winning a muffin basket."

"Here, here!" They turned to see Caleb and Jade approaching.

"How are you feeling?" Jade asked Greta.

"Lucky…and sore-legged. But mainly lucky. I feel a salon trip or a muffin basket is right here on this card." She tapped her bingo card with an index finger.

"I hope you're right," Jade said.

"If you are, will you share your muffins?" Caleb asked.

"Of course."

"I donated a box of truffles," Cade said. "I thought it would be a good way to introduce myself to some of the residents."

Greta winked and nodded. "I'm Mr. Carson's head of marketing. I get paid in candy."

"Big mouth," Steve said. "Now, we'll have to share our candy too."

"Um…excuse me."

Greta's gaze slid to Joanne as Eve Wallace approached them.

"Hi, Eve," Joanne said.

"Joanne." She nodded at Joanne and then at Andrew. "I'd like to introduce you to my daughter Amber."

Amber was a lovely blonde girl who, quite frankly, could've been Joanne's sister. She was also very pregnant—about eight months along, if Greta wasn't mistaken.

"Hi, Joanne." Amber extended a hand. "Mom told me about how she'd met you and your grandmother. In fact, it was your grandmother who invited us here tonight. She said I might win something cute for the baby or something nice—like a pedicure—for myself." Amber laughed. "I'd love a pedicure. I can't even see my feet these days."

"It's such a pleasure to meet you," Joanne said.

An announcer told everyone to get their cards ready, and Eve told Amber they'd better find a seat.

As they walked away, Joanne arched a brow at Greta. "You're always up to something, you know that?"

Greta shrugged. "What can I say? It runs in our family."

###

HAVE YOU READ THE FIRST BOOK IN THE *KINSEY FALLS* SERIES?
Excerpt from *HIGHTAIL IT TO KINSEY FALLS*

Chapter One

A S MILLIE WALKED OUT of the Community Center, she was making a mental list of the things she needed from the grocery store. She didn't need much: coffee pods, dishwashing detergent, tea pods—she certainly didn't need a baby possum.

But there it was, lying in the sun at the side of the walk. At least, that's what she thought it was. She stepped over into the grass and leaned closer. The gray-and-white creature with the tiny pink paws and tail looked as if it were trying to disappear into the ground. It opened its wide mouth and emitted a harmless little hiss at her.

"Oh, poor baby." Yep. It was a possum.

Millie saw no sign of its mother or any siblings, but there were too many dogs and cats around to leave the poor thing to fend for itself. She rifled through her purse until she found her makeup bag. She emptied the bag into the purse, sat the purse on the ground beside her, and proceeded to use the now-empty canvas bag to capture the baby possum. Once the possum was inside the bag, she quickly zipped it closed, leaving a small breathing hole.

Millie grabbed her purse and hurried back into the building. The pet shop was located right beside Nothin' But Knit, and she hoped Jade and Terri wouldn't spot her. How in the world would Millie explain to her granddaughter that she had a possum in her makeup bag?

The bell over the door of Hightail It! Pet Supply and Grooming jingled when Millie went inside.

"Be right with you," a male voice called.

"Hurry, please!" Millie placed her purse on the counter so she could hold the cosmetic bag with both hands. The possum didn't appear to be moving. She'd like to have unzipped the bag just a bit more, but she'd prefer to wait until the professional arrived.

A muscular young man came out of the stockroom with a fifty-pound bag of dog food on his shoulder. He eased the bag onto the floor and smiled at Millie. "Someone called and requested we have this bag ready for pickup today. Was that you?"

This guy was really handsome. Thick, wavy dark hair with a bit of a curl to it…deep chocolate-colored eyes…excellent build shown off to perfection in a white tee shirt and nicely fitting jeans… Had Jade met him?

Millie realized she was staring and smiled. "Nope. Not me."

He returned her smile. "What can I do for you then?"

"I have a… Well, I was going to my car, and I found this…this…." She held the makeup bag toward the young man.

He took it gingerly. "What've you got in here—a bird?"

"It's a…possum."

That sent his eyebrows skyward. "Huh. Well, let's see what we can do. Be right back." He carefully put the bag on the counter before sprinting back to the stockroom. He returned with a small, square box with high enough sides that, hopefully, the possum wouldn't escape and run amok in the shop.

Handsome held the bag inside the box and slowly unzipped it. "Hmm…" He gently turned the bag onto its side and dumped the tiny body into the box.

As soon as the young man moved his head, Millie peered inside. "Oh, no! Is it dead? Did I kill it?"

"No. I believe what you're seeing is called tonic immobility." He held up the makeup bag by his index finger and thumb. "I do think you're gonna want to replace this, though. Your new buddy left you a not-so-pleasant present."

"Ugh…yeah. Could you get rid of that bag for me?"

He laughed. "Sure. I'll throw it in our dumpster out back." In the meantime, he double-bagged it. "I'm Caleb, by the way."

"Millie." She sighed. "Bless its heart—I didn't mean to scare it. It's just a baby. I was trying to mount a rescue."

"I know." He seemed to shrug off her bringing a possum into his shop as if it were an everyday occurrence.

"Do you live upstairs?" Millie asked.

"I do," he said. "You?"

"Yep…other side of the hall from you, I'm sure."

"Nah! Really? How'd you get stuck over there with the golden oldies?" He grinned.

"Just lucky, I guess." She looked around the pet shop. She didn't have any pets of her own and had never been inside. "This is a nice place. Is it yours?"

"No, I'm just working here while getting my graduate degree in urban and regional planning."

"That sounds…" She shrugged. "It sounds confusing. What is it?"

"It's basically coming up with stuff like this Community Center," he said. "This is the type of designing I want to do. Take things in danger of being discarded and make them useful and new again."

The Kinsey Falls Living and Retail Community Center was the brainchild of an innovative real estate developer who had taken a dying mall and had turned it into a community that catered to two specific groups—seniors and young professionals. The upstairs had been converted to micro-apartments with the "golden oldies" on the left side and the YPs on the right. The retail spaces downstairs were designed to appeal to both groups as well as to the general public. There were common areas both upstairs and down, and community gardens were located at the right and left sides of the building.

"Don't let some of those golden oldies hear you say that. They'd take it as a challenge."

"You think?"

"I know. I imagine there are several of the women who'd try to give Mrs. Caleb a run for her money."

He arched a brow. "Are you fishing, Millie?"

"A little," she admitted. "My single granddaughter owns the knitting shop right next door to you. Pretty redhead. Have you noticed her in here?"

"I haven't...and I'm sure I'd remember a pretty redhead. You think I should take up knitting?"

"Maybe you should. It's very relaxing...or so they tell me."

"You don't knit?"

"Heavens, no." She grinned. "Maybe I will one day...when I'm a golden oldie." She nodded at the box. "How long before we know if Baby Possum is alive or in-intoxicated...or whatever you called it?"

"Tonic immobility. It could last up to four hours."

"Goodness! It'll take that long to determine whether it's alive or not?"

"Hopefully not," Caleb said. "In the meantime, I'll call the one of the local veterinarians to see how we should proceed."

"Well, if the poor possum is still alive and the vet will treat it, I'll take it to the animal hospital." She shrugged. "I feel responsible for little...Perry."

"Perry?"

"Yeah…that sounds like a good unisex name…don't you think?"

Caleb laughed. "Perry the possum, it is."

Millie took a card out of her purse. The black-and-gold card had Millicent Fairchild in bold, elegant letters in the middle of the card and her cell phone number in a smaller font below her name. She'd taken an online printing company up on their offer of free business cards after she'd gotten her phone. She handed the card to Caleb. "Please let me know when Perry wakes up."

"I will, Millie. And I'll let you know what the vet says too."

"Thanks." She smiled to herself as left the store. Caleb was handsome, kind, educated…he could be a great match for Jade. Millie wasn't thinking about happily ever after for Jade, like her daughter Fiona was, but she could see that Jade was lonely. A little male companionship would do her granddaughter good.

* * *

Jade put the blue cat carrier onto the hot-pink countertop at Nothin' But Knit and let Mocha out into the shop. Mocha, a seal point Himalayan, was a fixture in the store. He strolled out of the carrier, bumped Terri on the chin with his large head, and hopped down onto the oak hardwood floor to wind around Jade's feet. Jade sat the carrier beneath the counter.

It was already seventy-five degrees on this Saturday morning, and Jade was glad the Community Center had excellent air conditioning. Terri, Jade's business partner and best friend since middle school, was making sure the shop was tidy before unlocking the doors. The shop—and, in fact, the entire Kinsey Falls Living and Retail Community Center—had only been open for a few weeks. The grand opening celebration was being held a week from today.

"You're going to teach this loom class, aren't you?" Terri asked, brows furrowing together over wide brown eyes. "You know I don't do great with kids."

"Aw, come on," Jade said. "This experience would be good for you."

"No, it wouldn't."

Jade laughed as her grandmother Millie waltzed into the shop and did a three-sixty spin.

"How do y'all like my new duds?" She wore a black, pink, and white floral-print maxi skirt with a fuchsia v-neck tee. Like Jade, Millie had once been a redhead, but now her hair was a silvery white.

"That's a gorgeous outfit," Terri said. "But I thought you had a moratorium on new clothes for the time being."

The moratorium was because the micro-apartments upstairs didn't have a great deal of storage space.

"I do. And the other gals do too. That's why some of us got together and decided to host a swap meet in the atrium. We're going to have one each month and trade off," Millie said. "And not just clothing, but scarves, bags, and jewelry too."

"How fun!" Jade kissed Millie's cheek. "My smart, sexy grandma."

"You got that right. You gals are welcome to come to the next one. We're trying to get as many people involved as possible." She smoothed out her skirt. "Now, what were you saying would be a good experience for Terri? Y'all know how I hate missing stuff."

"Yep, Grandma, you've got serious FOMO."

"Fear of missing out," Terri explained to a bewildered Millie. "She's trying to get me to teach the tween girls' loom class."

"One of the girls' moms booked the class as part of the child's birthday celebration." Jade placed eight looms on the counter. "She bought each one a loom and is buying them the yarn to make a scarf."

"Gee whiz. When your mother was little, we just had a cake," said Millie. "When you were little, your mother sent everybody off with goodie bags full of candy and cheap toys. Today, the moms are buying looms and yarn for whole parties full of kids? Sounds like an expensive takeaway to me."

"It's all about the experiences," Jade said. "Sure, people today want stuff, but they want experiences even more. Well, you get it, Grandma…or else you wouldn't live at the Community Center."

Millie shrugged. "Experience, my foot. I don't see why they can't share a loom."

"For one thing, they can't all make a scarf on one loom at the same time. And for another, they can't share a loom because that's bad for our business," Terri pointed out.

"She's got you there, Grandma." Jade carried the looms into the knitting room and spaced them out evenly on the large round table. The table had been a flea-market find and had a distressed white finish. The armless chairs had been upholstered in pink-and-purple paisley.

"Also, there's no way the girls can finish their scarves in the allotted time," Jade called from the knitting room. "They'll need to take their looms and yarn home to complete them. What are your plans for the rest of the day?" She ran her palms down the sides of her jeans as she returned to the main part of the shop.

"After I leave here, I'm going to pick up a few essentials at the grocery store. When I get back and put my groceries away, I'll go to the pet shop and check on Perry."

"Who's Perry?" Terri asked.

"Perry is a…a baby…animal…that I found outside this morning and took over to the pet shop. Have you gals met Caleb? He works in the pet shop and is absolutely dreamy."

"Wait, who are Perry and Caleb again?" Jade asked.

Millie blew out a breath. "Weren't you listening? Caleb is the gorgeous guy who works at the pet shop. He's a real sweetheart too."

"And you met him how?" Jade frowned. Her grandmother didn't even own a pet. What was she doing visiting the pet shop?

"I met him when I took Perry, the rescued animal, to him," Millie said. "He's helping me make sure Perry is safe."

Jade ran a hand across her brow. "And what kind of animal is

119

Perry?"

"Perry is a possum."

Terri laughed. "Perry, the possum! That's cute!"

"Grandma! You picked up a freaking possum? Are you out of your mind?"

"I didn't pick up the possum...exactly. I kinda scooped it into my makeup bag."

"Ewww!" Jade threw both hands up to the sides of her head "Grandma, that's nasty! You've got to throw all that makeup away—"

"Jade, please. I certainly didn't put a possum in my makeup bag with my makeup still in it. Besides, Caleb threw the bag away and put Perry in a box until he or she comes out of..." She couldn't remember the term. "Until the possum wakes up."

"Oh. My. Gosh. Grandma, please tell me you didn't take a dead possum into the pet shop to have them try to save it!"

Terri was doubled over with laughter. "This...is...great!"

"Terri, hush," Jade scolded. "It's not great. It's...it's horrible. Grandma, that guy will think you're nuts."

"I'm not nuts, nor does Caleb think I am. The possum was alive when I scooped him up, and Caleb believes Perry is still alive. In fact, he's going to call me when Perry wakes up."

Wiping tears from the corners of her eyes, Terri asked, "Who's going to call you—Caleb or Perry?"

Millie cut Terri a disapproving glance and then addressed Jade. "I'm not as loopy as you two seem to think I am." She looked around the shop until she spotted Mocha. "Aw, there's my boy! He doesn't judge!" She went over to pet him. "The young people are having a pre-grand opening mixer in the atrium tonight. You two should go. Maybe gorgeous Caleb will be there."

"He sounds wonderful," Terri said. "This knight in shining— what? Denim, maybe? Saving possums and making women swoon."

Terri lived in one of the apartments upstairs. Jade lived in the house Millie had sold her when she'd moved into her apartment.

Millie had chosen the simplicity and socialness of "Community Center life" to continuing to maintain a house.

Since Jade didn't live at the Community Center, she didn't feel comfortable attending the gathering. Besides, she had a sneaking suspicion that her mother was behind Grandma's attempts to cajole her into attending the party and singing the praises of Mr. Pet Shop. Next, she'd be asking Grandma to leave job listings for Jade by the cash register.

Jade's mother thought Jade was wasting her time with a knitting shop. "Too much work and not enough profit." In Mom's opinion, Jade either needed to find a more lucrative career or a rich husband. Jade wasn't in the market for either. She was doing fine, thank-you-very-much.

Seeing that Jade didn't seem to plan on responding to Millie, Terri said, "We'll think about it. Thanks for reminding us."

Jade pointed to the flyers she'd printed out yesterday afternoon. "Terri, don't let me forget to put those flyers up in the library, café, and atrium when I take my lunch break. I already have the information on the Community Center app for the YPs, but I'm afraid the seniors won't see it there."

Millie sniffed. "You act as if we old fogies don't even know what an app is."

"Do you use the app, Grandma? Did you see the information about the beginning knitters' class on there?"

"I prefer to get my news the old-fashioned ways—like newspapers, televisions, and community bulletin boards." She stiffened her back and raised her chin. "But I do know what an app is and how to use it if I'm so inclined."

"We know, Millie," Terri said. "You're cooler than most of the other seniors around here."

"Yes, well…"

That was Millie's way of shrugging off a compliment.

As her grandmother left, Jade turned to Terri. "Did she really just come in here and tell us she rescued a possum that might or might not be living?"

Terri nodded.

She blew out a breath and looked around the shop. The white floor-to-ceiling blocks contained various colors and types of yarn. An oak stepladder on wheels stood waiting by the window for someone to need something from a top shelf. A padded navy bench sat in front of the window and was a wonderful place to knit when things got slow in the shop. Those moments didn't happen often, but Jade appreciated them when they did. In fact, she wished she could sit down now and process what had happened. She really needed to talk to that pet shop guy and try to explain to him that Grandma wasn't crazy. Sure, she could be a little ditzy now and then...forgetful sometimes...but not crazy. Definitely not crazy...although putting a possum in a makeup bag was pretty nutso.

Terri interrupted Jade's reverie. "Here they come."

Jade had no idea why children struck such fear in her petite blonde friend's heart, but she was having fun playing on that fear this morning. "Wish me luck."

"See you on the other side."

The eight girls came squealing into the shop. Jade introduced herself and had them tell her their names. She repeated them and made it a point to remember them.

"First, let's pick out your yarn."

"Is it all right if I go over and make sure everything is set up for their tea party at the café?" the mom asked, one foot already back out the door.

"That's fine," Jade said. "If I need you, I'll send Terri to get you."

"All righty. If I don't hear from you, I'll be back in an hour." She paused. "Will they be done in an hour? I can give you more time if you need it."

"An hour will be fine," Jade said firmly. "Their scarves won't be finished by then, but they'll be well on their way and the girls will know how to complete them. Should they need any help, they can always come back."

* * *

Jade was more frazzled than she'd expected to be when the girls finally galloped off to the café with the birthday girl's mom.

"That was an excellent sale," Terri said.

"I earned every penny of it. From the cast-on row to explaining that fringe was a little too advanced for them on this project." She looked around. "Where's Mocha?"

"He hid when the girls stormed in. I imagine he'll come out soon."

"Hidey-ho!"

"What I said about Mocha coming out? Scratch that," Terri said under her breath as Greta Parker blasted through the door.

Greta was a force of nature. She had short auburn hair with streaks of plum. Today she wore jeans and a baseball shirt bearing the logo for the group Imagine Dragons. Gold sparkly sneakers completed the outfit.

"I like your shirt," Jade said. "Are you a fan?"

"Oh, yes! Imagine if there were dragons." Greta put up her hands and spread them out slowly as if to illustrate the magnitude of such an idea. "Like in that show everyone is wild over. I haven't got to see it yet. I'm waiting to have enough time to binge it."

Nope. Just as Jade had suspected, Greta didn't realize Imagine Dragons was a music group. She thought it was a suggestion.

Terri jerked her head in the direction of the knitting room. "Are you gonna work a while? I'll be glad to help you get something from your project locker."

The knitting room contained four vertical cabinets. Each cabinet had four tiered spaces for a total of sixteen cabinets. At present, ten of the doors contained the name of regular patrons. Jade was sure they'd fill up once the shop had been open a bit longer.

"No, thanks, dolls," Greta said. "I'm looking for Millie. Have you seen her?"

"Not since this morning," Jade said. She decided not to tell Greta about the possum incident.

"Oh, well, I'll find her. And if you see her before I do, tell her I'm looking for her."

"Why don't you just call her?" Terri asked.

"I'm almost out of minutes." With that, Greta was gone.

"It's safe to come out now, Mocha," said Terri.

The cat obviously didn't believe her and remained in his hiding place.

"Don't be so hard on Greta," Jade said. "She's...well, she's unique."

"I know. It's just that she and I are the senior and YP liaisons for the grand opening celebration, and I feel like she isn't doing enough for the seniors. She's trying her best to be a millennial, and it ain't happening."

* * *

Ready to read the rest?
https://www.amazon.com/dp/B07C46H3WH

Recipes

Easy French Crepes
www.sweetashoney.co/french-crepes-recipe-easy/

Doctored Up Chocolate Cake Mix
www.thefirstyearblog.com/doctored-up-chocolate-cake-mix/

Chicken Fried Steak and Gravy
www.foodnetwork.com/recipes/ree-drummond/chicken-fried-steak-with-gravy-recipe-1925056

About the Author:

Gayle Leeson is a pseudonym for Gayle Trent. I also write as Amanda Lee. As Gayle Trent, I write the Daphne Martin Cake Mystery series and the Myrtle Crumb Mystery series. As Amanda Lee, I write the Embroidery Mystery series.

The cake decorating series features a heroine who is starting her life over in Southwest Virginia after a nasty divorce. The heroine, Daphne, has returned to her hometown of Brea Ridge to open a cake baking and decorating business and is wrestling with the question of whether or not one can go home again. She enjoys spending time with her sister, nephew, and niece, but she and her mother have a complicated relationship that isn't always pleasant. Daphne has also reconnected with her high school sweetheart and is pursuing a rekindled romance while desperately trying to put her past behind her.

Kerry Vincent, Hall of Fame Sugar Artist, Oklahoma State Sugar Art Show Director, and Television Personality says the series is "a must read for cake bakers and anyone who has ever spent creative time in the kitchen!"

Says Dean Koontz, #1 New York Times bestselling author, "One day I found myself happily reading . . . mysteries by Gayle Trent. If she can win me over . . . she's got a great future."

The Embroidery Mystery series features a heroine who recently moved to the Oregon coast to open an embroidery specialty shop. Marcy Singer left her home in San Francisco, along with the humiliation of being left at the altar, in order to move to Tallulah Falls and realize her dream of owning her own shop. She takes along her faithful companion, a one-year-old Irish wolfhound named Angus O'Ruff. She makes many new friends in Tallulah Falls, but she also makes a few enemies. Thankfully, her best friend Sadie MacKenzie and her husband Blake run the coffeehouse right down the street from Marcy's shop, the Seven-Year Stitch; and Detective Ted Nash always has her back.

Publishers Weekly says, "Fans of the genre will take kindly to Marcy, her Irish wolfhound, Angus O'Ruff, and Tallulah Falls. This is a fast, pleasant read with prose full of pop culture references and, of course, sharp needlework puns."

Pat Cooper of RT Book Reviews says, "If her debut here is any indication, Lee's new series is going to be fun, spunky and educational. She smoothly interweaves plot with her character's personality and charm, while dropping tantalizing hints of stitching projects and their history. Marcy Singer is young, fun, sharp and likable. Readers will be looking forward to her future adventures." (RT Book Reviews nominated The Quick and the Thread for a 2010 Book Reviewers' Choice Award in the Amateur Sleuth category)

I live in Virginia with my family, which includes my own "Angus" who is not an Irish wolfhound but a Great Pyrenees who provides plenty of inspiration for the character of Mr. O'Ruff. I'm having a blast writing this new series!

The Kinsey Falls series is a departure from the cozy mysteries most of my readers know me for, but I wanted to write a character-driven series that didn't always focus on murders. Don't despair if you prefer the mysteries, though! I'm currently at work on a new cozy series called The Ghostly Fashionista Mystery Series. That series features a designer of retro fashions whose studio comes with its own vintage ghost—a woman who died in 1930. Stay tuned…

Made in the USA
Middletown, DE
09 November 2018